CAT HOUSE

*A CRAZY
CAT LADY
MYSTERY*

BY MOLLIE HUNT

Cat House, the 10th Crazy Cat Lady mystery
by Mollie Hunt

All rights reserved. This book or any portion thereof may not be reproduced or used in any manner whatsoever without the express written consent of the author except for the use of brief quotations in a book review.

ISBN: 9798852898555
Independently published

Copyright 2023 © Mollie Hunt

Editing and Design by Rosalyn Newhouse

Published in the United States of America

No generative AI has been used in the conceptualization, development, or drafting of this work.

This book is a work of fiction. Names, characters, places, and incidents either are products of the author's imagination or are used fictitiously. Any resemblance to actual events or locales or persons, living or dead, is purely coincidental.

Cover Art: "Fireside Cat"
© 2002 by Leslie Cobb, Cat Artist
www.lesliecobb.com

Other Books by Mollie Hunt

Crazy Cat Lady Mysteries
Cats' Eyes
Copy Cats
Cat's Paw
Cat Call
Cat Café
Cat Noel
Cosmic Cat
Cat Conundrum
Adventure Cat
Cat's Play
Cat House

The Tenth Life Cozy Mysteries
Ghost Cat of Ocean Cove
Ghost Cat on the Midway

Other Mysteries
Placid River Runs Deep

Poetry
Cat Poems: For the Love of Cats

Cat Seasons Sci-Fantasy Tetralogy
Cat Summer
Cat Winter
Cat Autumn

Dedication

This book is dedicated to the FIP Warriors and their families; to all the scientists and doctors who are working to find cures for horrendous diseases like *feline infectious peritonitis*; and to the people like you and me who can help, dollar by dollar, to fund the necessary research to get this done.

Acknowledgements

Sincere thanks to Peter Cohen, founder of ZenByCat, a nonprofit dedicated to raising both awareness and money to help fight against FIP and save cat's lives. Peter is also the owner of the most catified home in California, House of Nekko.

Thanks also to Leslie Cobb for her story of Otis (*Otis the Alien*, as his 6000 Facebook followers call him) and his journey through FIP treatment. If it hadn't been for her encouragement to include a storyline with a cat being treated for FIP, this would have been a different book.

You can read more about both Otis and Peter in the afterword.

THREE YOUNG MEN HAD GONE MISSING from the Seattle-Portland corridor over the previous two months. The police had no clues and nothing to tie the victims to each other aside from their age—early twenties. There had been no ransom notes, no signs of a struggle. Nothing had been stolen from their homes. They were there one day, business as usual, and the next day they were gone. No one heard from them; there was no activity on credit cards or cell phones. Abducted by aliens or nefarious humans? It was still anyone's guess.

Chapter 1

The term "Crazy Cat Lady" can carry an offensive connotation, but it can also be a term of endearment between cat people. And by the way, there are Crazy Cat Men as well.

I'd walked by that strange little house a hundred times—the boxy front yard populated with plaster gnomes and fairies, the dream catchers floating from the eaves. Wind chimes jangled in discordant tattoos—bamboo, pipe, and glass. Those oddities had caught my eye, but what held it were the cats.

In the front window, they lounged on perches and in cat trees. Within the safety of a small covered catio even more prowled and jumped. Sometimes I'd try to count them but would get stuck when the black one would disappear behind a cushion, only to reappear as twins, or the tuxedo would turn in his bed, revealing a whole new cat underneath. Yes, there was a reason why the locals called the resident of 59th and Main a crazy cat lady.

My name is Lynley Cannon, and I've been tagged with that moniker a few times myself. More than a few, to be honest. As a single woman in her sixties with nine cats in my home, I saw how someone might draw that conclusion.

Dirty Harry was the oldest, quickly approaching the big seventeen. Black floofy Tinkerbelle was getting up there as well, but you'd never know it by her activity level. She, Little, and Emilio were my black cat trio, and when they curled up together, they looked like a black hole in space. Shy Big Red and gorgeous Hermione were tabbies, as was Elizabeth, my "wobbly" cat. Violet was gray and white and shaped like a beachball. Mab, the youngest of the group, was a purebred Siamese.

So, the *cat woman* part I readily accepted—it was the *crazy* part that gave me pause. I'm not crazy, at least not yet.

So who was this kindred soul, this rival for the status of cat lady living around the block from me? I'd never met her, never even seen her, but that was about to change.

It started with an ad on the Friends of Felines bulletin board from someone looking for a cat sitter. I'm not sure why her flyer caught my eye—it was in no way distinctive, a paragraph of text in a plain black font, and two photos. One was a picture of cats, at least six of them, all lined up on a stark white sofa. The other was of a house I recognized—the Cat House 59th and Main.

On a whim, I'd answered. I don't know what drove me to do it. I wasn't looking for a job. I suppose it had been curiosity. Like the cat in the age-old proverb, curiosity was my downfall, and as with that unfortunate feline, the only thing that will satisfy the itch is to jump in feet first. Too many times I've thrown caution to the wind in order to discover who, what, or why.

But this was only a little cat sitting gig—the chance of misfortune was slim, or so I'd thought. The fact that the flyer had been up on the bulletin board for over a month with no takers should have served as a warning.

Chapter 2

The best way to keep your cats happy is to provide them with an Environment of Plenty. In other words, ensure they have enough food stations, water bowls, beds, hidey-holes, climbers, and toys for all to enjoy without squabbling.

My questions about cat sitting for Darla of 59th and Main Street would be answered soon enough—I was set to meet the infamous cat lady later that day. She'd told me very little in her brief text, but that was okay. She'd been gracious, polite, and used punctuation, all of which I considered a good sign. How much could one really say in a text anyhow? Better face to face where a two-way conversation could bring enlightenment without the considerable use of thumbs.

In the meantime, I was at my kitchen sink, rinsing a few dishes and wondering if I should change out of my daywear sweats into something less casual. What would be appropriate for a cat-sitting interview? A cat-themed sweater? Cat-patterned socks? I figured my sparkly cat ears might be a bit much, but who knew, when the person I was meeting kept a bevy of gnomes in her front yard?

I was coming to the conclusion I was overthinking the issue when I caught movement outside my window. Glancing up, I started. A large sunflower was making its way across my back yard. It disappeared onto the patio, and I heard a tap on my back door.

Drying my hands, I adjusted my glasses, briefly

wondering if I had been seeing things. When I opened the door to the tall, stately plant, I was reassured.

"Hi, Lynley," said the flower, raising its leaves and flashing a wide smile. "What do you think? Am I not a resplendent Helianthus?"

"If that means sunflower, then yes, Fredric, you are all that and more."

I stood back as the young man in the flower costume shuffled inside. The green tubing that sheathed his body from neck to feet inhibited his usually assertive stride, and he stumbled.

"Shoot!" I heard him mumble as he righted himself. "Still needs a few modifications, I guess."

"I'd say so." I closed the door and followed him into the kitchen. "If you plan to do any walking, that is."

He bent over and hiked the skirt up to his knees. "You're right about that. Seleia's got me passing out flyers for the play at the All-Hallows fête."

"Well, I suppose you could *plant* yourself in one spot and hand them out from there." I laughed at my pun, and so did Fredric.

Fredric Delarosa, my granddaughter Seleia's beau, may have been a few generations younger than me, but we were kindred spirits just the same. When not dressed as a sunflower, he was a tall young man, good looking and getting more so as he aged. Dusky-red hair, hazel eyes, with always an easy smile, caused me to worry at first that his bright disposition was a façade, acquired in the film business he'd grown up around, but over time it had proven genuine. He was a confident, intelligent, outgoing person, and I was happy to have him as a friend.

I was equally pleased he lived in the vintage duplex across the street from me and was willing to help an older woman in times of need. My big Victorian house sometimes proved more than I could manage alone. Fredric had fixed the fence, pruned the wisteria, installed air conditioning during the unbearably hot summer, and more. Knowing there was someone who was able to do the things I couldn't was a great relief.

"Hopefully it doesn't rain," he commented, continuing to adjust his costume.

"This is Portland, Fredric. It always rains on Halloween. It's tradition."

"There are exceptions to every rule, Lynley," the young man retorted. "Maybe this will be one."

I finished rinsing the last few dishes, pulled out the rubber plug—yes, my sink is that old—and watched the water slurp down the drain. "How's the play coming? Seleia won't tell me anything. She says she wants it to be a surprise."

"Well! Very well. Seleia's a natural for the part of Hermia. She says she's never acted before, but that can't be true."

"It is." I thought about my granddaughter through her nineteen years growing up—I was there every step of the way. "And I would know."

Fredric rolled up his leafy sleeves and pushed back the sunflower hoodie. "Is she around?"

"She's in the studio with Carol. They're working on posters."

Fredric raised an eyebrow. "Your mother is helping?"

"Sure. Carol did set design back in the day. She's quite an artist, though she only does it for fun."

"Huh," Fredric muttered. "I had no idea."

"Just because she's eighty-five doesn't mean she's past it."

"That wasn't what I meant. It's just that I never pictured Carol as the creative type. Mostly all she and her roommate talk about are food and old detective series reruns."

I sighed. "You have a point there."

"Well, I'm going to find Seleia. I want her to check out my costume. She'll be the final judge, of course."

Fredric headed for the studio, the place I'd outfitted to do my miscellaneous projects. Living as the only human in a fourteen-room house had allowed me to turn extra bedrooms into whatever I pleased. A place where I could spread out and be creative had been second on the list—first on the list was making the environment friendly for my cats.

Speaking of cats, I noted several pairs of eyes tracking my movement as I followed Fredric through the house. Furry heads rose momentarily, then sank back onto paws and breasts as if we weren't worthy of disturbing an afternoon nap.

"Fredric's here," I called ahead.

Seleia poked her head out of the studio, pleasure flashing across her face like a light. She gave the boy a chaste peck on the cheek, appropriate for the family audience, then led him into the big room with a giggle of glee.

A wall of shelves stocked with art and craft items, a cupboard full of paints, and a big drafting table made it the perfect place to follow whatever creative whim might come, and that current whim was an array of brightly painted signs in various states of production. Vividly colored text read: *A Brief Snippet of A Mid-Autumn Night's Dream, by Kiefer Clark with a nod to William Shakespeare*—a catchy title for the parody of the master's work, rewritten by a local playwright who by no coincidence was also the director.

"Wow!" both Fredric and I exclaimed as our gaze swept the collection.

"Well?" posed a small, aged figure with a paint brush in her hand and a streak of purple running from her tight gray curls to her wrinkled cheek—my mother Carol. "What do you think?"

Carol Mackay may have been in her mid-eighties, and surely she looked it, but no one had told her spirit, which bloomed with vibrance and enthusiasm. The way she smiled at me now, purple not included, was more like that of a roguish teen than a woman past a certain age.

"Nicely done! If these don't inspire people to come to the show, nothing will."

Carol slipped out from behind the drawing board and gave Seleia a little sideways hug. "We make a good team, don't we, dear?"

"We certainly do! I couldn't have done it without you, Granna."

"I should hope not!" my mother retorted with shameless egotism.

Two larger placards of a different theme caught my eye. "Who are the Terrace Traders?"

"That's me," Carol said. "Or I should say, that's us. A group from the Terrace rented a booth at the Hawthorne All-Hallows Fête."

"A booth?" I tried to imagine what a bunch of old folks from my mother's assisted living facility would sell in a booth.

"Why not? Make some extra cash? We're all on fixed incomes, you know."

I happened to know they weren't, since the monthly

rent at the Terrace was more than anyone's social security check alone could handle, but I didn't balk.

"Just kidding, love. We're actually planning to give most of it to your cat shelter, for the cats."

"Oh," I exclaimed, knowing Friends of Felines would appreciate the gift, even though it might only be a few pennies. "That's great. Thanks for thinking of us."

"We're really quite an innovative bunch. Everything for sale will be handmade—silk flowers, Christmas decorations, afghans, soaps and lotions, a bit of pottery…"

"I get the idea," I interrupted before she could list their entire inventory. "I suppose you'll need help setting it up."

"That would be wonderful, dear. I appreciate your volunteering."

Carol's eyes swept past me to Fredric, and her brows furrowed. "What are you wearing, young man?"

"It's my Halloween costume." He adjusted the sleeves and replaced the yellow-petaled headpiece. "I'm a sunflower," he stated unnecessarily.

"Of course you are," said Carol. "Forgive me for not seeing it before. But you'll have to do something about those legs," she tut-tutted. "Flowers don't have knobby white knees."

Fredric glanced down self-consciously. "There's more stem, but it makes it hard to walk so I rolled it up," he defended. "Knobby? Really?"

"I think they're just fine," Seleia put in, "but Carol's right—they don't really work with the rest of the costume. Maybe green tights?"

"And what are you going as?" I asked Seleia.

She skipped over to a tote on the sideboard and pulled out an elaborate headdress with furry orange and black stripes and black antennae draped with a veil of Spanish lace. Plopping it on her head, she turned back.

"I'm the bee."

"Ah, the flower and the bee!"

At least she's the bee and not the flower, I thought to myself, still protective of my sweet granddaughter's innocence. Though the girl was in her second year at college, to me she would always be a child.

"I was about to make some tea," I put in. "Can I entice you hard workers into a cup?"

"Perfect," Carol replied. "It's time for a break, right after Seleia and I clean up."

"I'll wash out the brushes," Seleia offered.

"And I'll supervise." Carol winked. "You two go on. We'll meet you in the living room."

Fredric and I left Seleia and Carol to their chore and went back to the kitchen where Fredric gathered tea things on a tray as I prepared the pot. I chose genmaicha as I knew everyone liked the Japanese green brew. By the time Fredric carried the tray through to the living room, Seleia was already settled on the loveseat with Dirty Harry, the eldest of my clowder. Carol had taken the easy chair and was swiping through her phone.

She frowned as she paused to read something. "There's been another one."

I poured tea into a squat blue cup with a cat face design and took it over to her. "Another what?"

"Another boy gone missing. That's the third. The news people are now saying the disappearances must be related."

"They aren't really boys, Mum," I corrected as I set the cup on the side table. "They're in their twenties, aren't they?"

Carol gave me a look. "Men, boys, all the same.

Whatever you want to call them, it's a crying shame."

"I thought they were runaways," said Fredric, pouring his own cup and inhaling the warm fragrance. "Guys who just took off for whatever reason."

"They don't think so." Carol scrolled a bit farther. "There's too much evidence that they've been taken. Is no one safe anymore?"

"But who would do such a thing?" queried Seleia, suddenly looking like the little girl she used to be. "And why?"

Carol and I were silent, the unspoken acknowledgement that women vanish all the time, while men are rarely a target.

Then Carol turned to Fredric who had gone to sit with Seleia. Her face grew dark as she studied the man.

"You'd better be careful, dear," she said in an ill-omened tone. "We wouldn't want you to be next."

Chapter 3

Affectionately known as Cat on Lap Syndrome, it's the predicament of not being able to get up and do something because the cat has taken to sitting on one's lap and we dare not disturb him.

With all the bad things going on in the world, I sometimes wondered if it would ever stop. This recent spate of abductions came way too close to home. Wars in foreign countries, even political affairs and climate change seemed so very far away from my cozy little neighborhood in southeast Portland, Oregon, but the three missing men had me worried. Thankfully no one had turned up dead. At least not yet.

I shook myself out of my morbid contemplation. I had other things to think about. It was nearly five o'clock, the time I'd agreed to meet my new cat-sitting client in the house around the corner. Though I'd cared for numerous cats, my own as well as other people's, I had never worked as an official paid cat sitter before. Still, I was confident I could handle it. I'd been volunteering in the Friends of Felines cattery for many years and taken classes in everything from litter box issues to chronic diseases. I'd even completed an online cat first-aid course for which I received a certification. The first rule, *don't panic*, would apply in just about any emergency, but hopefully none of the Cat House cats would require such ministrations.

What would they be like—those numerous felines I'd

spied through the window? How many were there? Seven? Ten? More? Darla hadn't mentioned it in her text. But then she hadn't mentioned a lot of things.

Our communication had been brief:

Me: Hello. My name is Lynley Cannon. I'm inquiring about your notice on the FOF bulletin board for a cat sitter.

Her: *Thank you for contacting me. Can you come to my house and meet the crew at 5:15 pm Tuesday? Address on the flyer.*

Me: Yes, I can do that. Is there anything I should know?

Her: *We'll talk then.*

Me: Wait—what's your name?

Her: *Darla.*

And that was it. Was she busy or was it a personal affectation? As the clock pinged five pm, I realized I would soon find out.

"I shouldn't be long," I told Seleia and Carol who were still working on posters in the studio. "Make yourselves at home."

"We will," Carol replied.

Darla's house was directly behind my mine, a few blocks up toward Mt. Tabor Park, and despite the gloomy autumn weather, I decided the walk would do me good. Bidding farewell to my own cats, I shrugged on a wool coat and slipped out the door. Though it wasn't raining at the moment, it could start anytime. Ducking back into the hallway, I grabbed a hat just in case.

I enjoyed the trek in the brisk, cold air. The wind had blown away some of the big city pollution, and now everything smelled like loam. So far, the autumn had been mild, leaving the flowers to bloom in a post-summer flurry—chrysanthemums, purple asters, even a few hardy roses showed buds on their straggly vines. A smattering of cars cruised the small back street, people returning home from work. The *thunk* of car doors and blip of automatic locks broke the urban hum, but for the most part, it was the beginning of a quiet night.

I rounded a corner, and the Cat House came into view. Though it was not yet sunset, the overcast created a false twilight, and against that gloom, the house glowed like something fit for a Hallmark movie. With its fairy lights in the catio and amber luminescence filtering through the front windows, nothing could have seemed cozier.

As I neared, I began to pick out cats lined up like sentries along the window ledge. They seemed to be watching me as I approached, as if they knew I was coming for them. Then a very large black one broke from the group and jumped up to the top of the cat tree. He settled in the basket, but his eyes were fixed on mine. He was absolutely gorgeous. I couldn't wait to meet him.

The front door swung open even before I'd made it onto the small covered porch, and in it stood a slight woman wearing a rainbow-colored tutu. Her hair was a cascade of magenta and orange curls, and her face was painted like an old-fashioned doll—round red dots on the cheeks and crimson Cupid's bow lips. Kohl-black lines surrounded bright blue eyes topped with a collage of eyeshadow in shades that defied identification.

She smiled, toying coyly with the tulle of her skirt. "You must be Lynley." Despite her waif-like appearance, her voice was deep and rich, reminding me of Kathleen Turner. "I'm Darla. Please come in."

I did as she bid, and she closed the door behind me, but not before leaning out to scour the scene.

"It's only me," I said, in case she was searching for a

companion.

"Oh, I just wanted to make sure there was no one following you. Can't be too careful. Of course, if they were crafty, they'd be hiding, and I wouldn't see them anyway. The crafty ones are the worst."

My instincts gave me a little nudge. Was Darla paranoid or did she have a reason to worry? One never knew these days. Either way, it wasn't a good sign. For a moment, I considered turning right around and heading back the way I'd come. Maybe this crazy cat lady really was crazy.

Then I felt a shimmer of warmth brush along my calf. I looked down to see the big black cat staring back up at me. He gave a slow blink, and my heart melted. Perhaps it didn't matter if Darla was a little bit on the wild side. I was there for the cats.

"Oscar likes you," she said, pulling aside a Japanese curtain and mincing into the living room on ballerina toes.

Oscar and I followed. After the lavishness with which she dressed herself, I expected to see a mishmash of kitsch, pop, goth, or hippie, and was surprised by the minimalistic one-room space done in shades of off-white and gray. Besides the row of cat trees in the front window, there was a Danish-style couch, a spindly light-wood coffee table, and a large red chair. The chair didn't fit with the décor, but I instantly saw its purpose—a pair of cats were curled on the well-clawed upholstery, and another stood on the back, in the process of adding even more tatters to the design.

Darla led me to a maple dining table on which several cat beds took precedence. One was occupied by a slim tabby, but the others were vacant. Darla nonchalantly swept all but one of the empties from the table and took a seat. Folding her hands and displaying a set of elaborately decorated fingernails, she smiled up at me.

"So you're a cat sitter?"

I sat in the chair opposite. "More like a cat *person*. I know a lot about cats."

"Mmmm."

The conversation stalled. Again I wondered why I was there since, no, I really wasn't a cat sitter. I wasn't licensed and bonded. I had no referrals, unless you talked to my own cats.

Then we both started at the same time:

"Maybe we should…"

"Let me begin by…"

This set off a round of *Go on*, and *No, you*, after which we both ended up laughing.

"I'm sorry," she said finally. "I'm not a great conversationalist. I've never hired a cat sitter before—or anyone, for that matter—and I guess I'm not sure where to start."

"That's okay," I said. "I haven't actually worked as a cat sitter, so we have something in common. But I do have lots of experience with cats." I lit into my resume of cat-related roles—shelter volunteer, therapy cat partner, my one gig helping a TNR group capture ferals for sterilization—and showed her pictures on my phone. "And I live around the block, so it would be really convenient for me to come, if you decide to hire me."

I wasn't sure when I'd made up my mind I wanted the job. Probably about the time Oscar jumped into my lap and gave me another series of love blinks.

But it wasn't my call.

"Mmmm, okay, that makes sense." Darla hesitated, then leapt from her chair and headed into the kitchen area.

"I'll be right back."

She returned moments later with a very old, very thin gray puss. She gently placed the cat in the empty bed, an especially soft plush one.

"This is Gloria."

Slowly, she pushed the bed in front of me. When the cat turned her face, I realized she was blind.

For a second time, I felt my heart melt. "Hello, sweetheart."

I gently reached out a hand to let her sniff. The cat paused, then pressed her face against my fingers. A soft purr emanated from her sinewy throat.

Shakily she stood and took a step toward me. I guided her onto my lap where she curled up beside Oscar as if she had always been there. It was a bit of maneuvering to hold both cats, but I managed. When I looked up at Darla, she was smiling.

"You're hired!"

I was stuck with COL, *Cat on Lap Syndrome*, or in this case, *Cats*, but that didn't stop Darla from going around the room and introducing the rest of her clowder. There was a Timmy and a Tommy, a Hans, a Freyja, a Webster and a Billy and a Léonard, but I really couldn't see all that well, and I'd never be able to pick them out in a test.

"Do any of them have medical issues, any medications I need to give?"

"Not really. I got a friend to come and do a topical flea treatment in July."

I frowned. "Shouldn't that be done monthly?"

She shrugged. "They're fine. I haven't seen anyone scratching."

"Anything else? Special diets?"

"They all eat the same thing—some premium kibble in

a blue bag that's supposed to make their coats shiny. It comes auto-ship, but I don't remember the name. Now that you mention it, I have been seeing some vomits. Do you think someone needs a special food?"

"Hard to say," I vagued. "Which one was throwing up?"

She stared at a tuxedo cat. "It was Tommy." But then she turned to the larger tuxie. "Or maybe it was Timmy. Sometimes I get them mixed up."

If you can't tell your own cats apart, I thought to myself, *how am I ever going to do it?*

"That's a lot of cats," I began. "It would help if you could give me pictures along with their names. I recently cared for a cat where the owner had made up a whole book about her—likes, dislikes, favorite spots, etc. It was really useful."

"What a good idea!" Darla exclaimed. "Yes, I'll do that for you. I'll have it ready by tomorrow when you come."

I did a double take. "Tomorrow? You want me to start tomorrow?"

"Yes. Is that a problem?"

I considered. "It depends on what you want me to do. We really haven't discussed that yet."

Darla reseated herself, smoothing her tutu which just fluffed right back out again, as is the nature of tulle.

"I need you to sit with them, let's say, what? Once a day for a few hours? There are treats on the kitchen counter. Everything else is automatic—the litter box, the food dispensers. There's a water fountain which might need cleaning if I'm gone for long."

"And will you be? Gone long?"

"I don't think so. This should be one night, two at the most. I'll text you when I know for sure."

She stood, and I thought the interview was over, but instead she said, "There is one more thing, Lynley."

"What's that?" I was thinking, bring in the mail or water a plant but instead she began to walk away.

"Please come with me."

I looked up in surprise, but she was serious, disappearing through the kitchen to a corridor at the back of the house. I returned Gloria to her bed and let Oscar jump down on his own, then followed.

Darla led me past a bathroom and a pair of bedrooms, stopping in front of a closed door at the far end of the hallway. The hall itself was painted a pale eggshell, but the door had been done in dark indigo blue. On it was hung a small framed painting of a seventeenth century demon. Under that was a roughly penned note that read, "No go in."

I looked at Darla, then reached for the doorknob.

"No, don't!" she cried. "Did you not see the sign?"

"Sorry. I thought this was what you wanted to show me."

"Exactly."

"But what's inside? Not really a demon, I presume."

"It's no concern. Just don't open the door. No matter what. Promise me, or the deal is off."

I paused, then said with a nervous stutter, "Ooo-kay, I promise." What else could I say?

Without another word, she retraced her steps down the hall back to the kitchen. I glanced again at the blue door, more curious than ever, then turned away.

"I'm sorry. I didn't mean…"

She eyed me for a moment, then smiled. "No problem, Lynley. Here's the house key." She produced a key on a lamp chain and handed it to me. Text if you have any questions. I'm always available."

With that she herded me toward the door.

"I really am sorry if I overstepped..." I said once outside.

She smiled again and touched my cheek, a strange gesture. "It's fine. You'll be fine. I'm so grateful you'll be watching the crew."

With that, she withdrew back inside and quickly closed the door. I stood on the little porch, staring at the cats through the window and wondering what I'd got myself into.

Chapter 4

Though cats seem aloof and independent, they don't do well on their own for extended periods of time. When going away for work or holiday, the best solution is to hire a reputable cat sitter to visit, or better yet, to stay the night.

Carol was still there when I returned from my cat-sitting interview, parked in front of the television set like she owned the place. The little woman with the big personality could give that impression, even to her daughter.

"What are you watching?" I asked as I shed my coat and hat and hung them in the hallway.

"Rockford. Shush."

Ah, my mum's heartthrob. She and her roommate Candy never seemed to tire of *The Rockford Files*, the dated who-done-it that played on the classic channel.

"Tea?" I asked, going through to the kitchen to make myself a cup.

"Yes please," she replied, followed by another shush sound.

I knew my place and quietly went about my business. It was only a bit after six, but the cats thought my presence heralded their dinnertime, and I found myself instantly surrounded. Lively meows ensued as the *nifty nine* jockeyed for position under my feet. I patiently explained that it wasn't time yet, and a few got the picture while others just sat, confused and waiting. I gave a pet to Hermione, my striking silver tabby with the unique paisley markings, who was nearest of the watchers, then returned to my task.

The *Rockford* episode was just winding up when I brought the tray into the living room. Carol turned to me in surprise.

"When did you get back?"

"I've been here for ten minutes," I countered. "I asked you if you wanted tea."

"Oh, of course." She shook her head. "I must have been distracted."

"I know you were. Gotta love that Rockford."

"Those were great shows," she exclaimed. "There's nothing like them anymore. Now it's all those mixed genre stories—sci-fi westerns and alien mysteries. How can a person keep track?"

"You like some of those shows, Mum," I countered. "All the new *Star Treks*?"

She sniffed. "Well, that's *Star Trek*. But enough." She picked her teacup from the tray, sniffed it, and took a sip. "How did your interview go? Did you get the job?"

I snorted. "Apparently. I start tomorrow."

"How many cats does she have?"

"I don't know exactly. A lot. I met two, and she pointed out the rest, but there were too many for me to keep track. She's going to leave me some pictures—I hope."

"That ought to keep you busy."

"Not really. Everything's automatic. She just wants me to drop in and socialize—make sure they're all okay."

I pondered for a moment. "Her name is Darla. She's young, mid-twenties at the most, and dresses like a clown princess. She seems nice enough…" I pushed the vision of the blue door to the back of my mind, "if a bit eccentric.

I'm not sure she knows as much about cats as…"

"As you do?" Carol finished for me.

"I was going to say, as she should when caring for so many. But it's okay, I guess—you don't have to be a behaviorist to take good care of your cats."

"What's she paying you?"

I hesitated, realizing Darla and I had never discussed compensation. "I suppose it depends on how long she's gone," I said ambiguously. If I admitted I'd taken a job without knowing how much it paid, I'd never hear the end of it.

"I hope this won't impact your helping with the booth."

Big Red, my sweet marmalade tabby, had taken up residence in the easy chair. I scooched the sleepy cat over and sat down beside him. "Booth?"

"The Terrace Traders. You promised you'd help us set up." She harrumphed. "Lynley dear, we were talking about it only an hour ago. I hope you're not starting to forget things."

"I remember. And I'm sure I'll have plenty of time for both. I can help you with the booth tomorrow afternoon. I don't have to start at the Cat House until the evening."

"Cat house?"

I laughed. "Darla's place. I've always called it that—ever since I started noticing all the cats in the window a few years ago."

Carol's phone gave a little chirp. She picked it off the coffee table and looked at the screen.

"That's Opal. She's outside waiting for me in the car." Carol grunted as she pulled herself up. "Gotta run, but I'll see you tomorrow at the hall, bright and early." She skewered me with an expectant stare.

"Bright and early in the *afternoon*," I corrected.

"Alright then."

I walked her to the door where she turned and gave me a hug. "About ten?"

With that as the last word, she turned away. I watched her shuffle down the steps and into Opal's vintage Cadillac. With a resigned sigh, I bid my mother farewell.

* * *

The Hawthorne All-Hallows Holiday Festival was something new for the neighborhood. Businesses up and down the eclectic boulevard were set to participate with sales, contests, giveaways, and special deals. The main event, a huge bazaar-style artisan's market, would take place in the old Masonic Hall. The Masons had sold the brick bastion to a developer years ago, and its many rooms and chambers had been converted for neighborhood use. The main hall, decorated in a medieval theme, would host the crafters and artists selling their wares in faux-primitive stalls. Other rooms would offer traditional Halloween favorites such as scary walk-throughs and pumpkin pie tasting, as well as provide playrooms and childcare for the attendees with small children. The culmination of the affair would come on Halloween afternoon when Kiefer Clark's long-titled parody play was presented in the auditorium.

That was where I found Seleia, Carol, and Fredric the next morning. Along with other young people, Fredric and Seleia were hard at work dragging the big sets on stage and arranging them in what seemed like no particular order. Carol was plopped down in a front row chair looking on as if she were the director.

I took the seat beside her, brushing my hand across the

timeworn puce plush.

"Remnants of a classical age," I commented.

"Who's a remnant?" Carol shot back. "Not me."

I laughed. "Good morning, Mum. How's it going?"

The octogenarian gave me a look up and down. "Morning? Is it still? Seems like I've been up for hours... Oh, right... that's because I have."

"I told you I wouldn't be here until later. What did I miss?"

"Not much." She gave a great sigh. "Turns out we can't set up the Terrace Traders booth until Thursday. I think that's running it close, since the festival opens on Friday, but that's what they said. Apparently other people have signed up to use the room until then."

"But today's only Sunday," I pointed out. "Whatever are you going to do in the meantime?"

"I'll be working here, of course."

"Working?" It was my turn to scoff.

Carol gestured to the hustle and bustle onstage as if I'd missed it. "Working."

Seleia breezed into the chair on my other side. Wearing a lavender leotard and leggings, she looked very much the actor.

"Hello, love." I patted her hand. "What are you up to this mid-morning?"

"Rehearsals and more rehearsals," she replied in all seriousness. "*Dream* may be a light comedy, but Mr. Clark takes it very seriously."

"*Dream*?" I commented.

"The original title's way too long to recite every time, so it got abbreviated to *A Mid-Autumn Night's Dream*, and then just *Dream*," Seleia explained.

"And are you enjoying yourself?"

"I'm loving it." She rose and gave a little twirl. "I had no idea how much I'd love acting! In fact," She paused, as if about to reveal the deepest of secrets. "I'm thinking of changing my major."

"Really?" I coughed. "From physics to drama? That's a big switch."

"I'll keep astrophysics as a minor. I doubt I'd ever be able to support myself on acting alone. But I can't pass up this chance to follow my dream."

"The acting bug has bit," Carol pronounced. "And once that happens, there's no getting away from it. I remember when I did *Our Town* back in high school…"

"You were in the theater too?" Seleia exclaimed excitedly.

"Oh, yes, my dear. You come by it naturally. The stage is in our blood." Carol gave Seleia's hand a conspiratorial squeeze.

"It must have bypassed me," I announced. "I've never done a lick of acting in my life. Never had the urge."

"That's not strictly true," Carol contradicted. "You dress up in your costumes and go to those comic book conferences of yours."

"That's not acting. I don't have to learn lines or anything."

"What is *Live long and prosper* or that Klingon word you're always uttering—*Ka-splat*—if not a form of script?"

"*Qapla'*," I shrugged. She had a point. I did love becoming someone else, some*thing* else, for a few hours. There were two types of people at those conventions: ones who dressed up and ones who didn't. The ones who dressed the part of a comic book character, superhero, furry, Disney princess, or whatever their heart desired were the ones who had the most fun.

Then we all laughed at our shared theatrical bent.

"Well, if I can't be of any use here," I said, "I should probably go to Friends of Felines and check on Mia and Frankie. They're the bonded pair I've been working with. Their person brought them in when she got sick and couldn't take care of them anymore. They'd lived with her all their lives and didn't know what hit them, so I'm trying my best to help them adjust to the shelter." I paused, running through my plans for the day. "After that, I'll be off to the Cat House."

Seleia furrowed her brow. "Cat house?" she asked, echoing my mother's query of the night before.

"Your grandmum got the job," Carol explained.

"That cat sitting gig you interviewed for yesterday?" I nodded. "But you didn't say it was at a cat house."

"It's just a house in my neighborhood," I began, realizing I needed to tell the whole tale if Seleia were to get the picture. "I noticed it a while back because it had an outdoor catio attached to the front facing. There were always cats inside, and every time I walked by, I'd try to count them. I never could come up with an accurate number, but once I made it up to ten. That's when I began calling it the Cat House. Then I saw the flyer at the shelter—someone looking for a cat sitter. It turned out to be at the same house!"

"Coincidence... or fate?" my mother posed.

"Maybe a little of both."

"Well, sounds like fun, Grandmother. Ten cats! That's even more than you have."

The call of a buzzer bell zinged through the auditorium, and Seleia snapped to attention. "I've got to get backstage. They're going to start rehearsals in a few minutes and Mr. Clark wants everyone on set." She pulled her long red hair into a ponytail which she affixed with a fabric tie she'd been wearing around her wrist. "What are you going to do, Granna?"

"I think I'll stay and watch for a while," said Carol. "Maybe give your director a bit of professional advice."

Seleia looked aghast.

"I'm just kidding, darling. I won't do anything to embarrass you, I promise."

Seleia gasped with relief, then bent down and gave her great grandmother a kiss on the cheek. "See you later, Granna. Lynley, good luck at your cat house."

Carol and I watched her bounce away and hop up onstage to join the huddle of actors.

"Proud, Mum?" I said aside.

"Extremely," she replied, her gaze never wavering from the lovely girl. "I hope she has as much fun in her life as I've had in mine."

"Really?" I turned to look at Carol. "You feel like you've had a fun life?"

"Of course, dear. Haven't you?"

I hadn't thought about my life in quite those terms before. Useful, yes. Productive, somewhat. Good, fair, honest… but fun? I equated fun with frivolity.

"Is fun even supposed to be a life goal?" I questioned.

"Of course it is," Carol replied without hesitation. "Other things are important, too, but without happiness we would all just wither and die."

Chapter 5

Adopting a kitten is both exciting and rewarding, but it comes with extra responsibilities to ensure the kitten thrives. You'll need to follow a strict feeding and health regimen as well as make sure those curious little beings don't get themselves into dangerous predicaments in their new home.

After visiting Mia and Frankie at the shelter and making sure they got some exercise and playtime outside their kennel, I headed home to get ready for my stint at the Cat House. Thinking about my new job gave me butterflies in my stomach, but they were good ones. I looked forward to getting to know Darla's *crew* better and to see fragile Gloria again. There was something about the tenacity of old cats that revitalized me. Gloria, despite being a senior and blind as well, had a great capacity for purrs and snuggles. There was something to learn from that.

I was just coming up onto my front porch when I heard my name called. I turned to find Fredric frantically waving at me through the front window of his duplex across the street. His voice was muffled, and I couldn't make out what he was saying. I assumed he would come outside and tell me, but instead he gestured for me to go there.

I hesitated a moment—I had things to do and was in a hurry to do them—but my curiosity was piqued. What could Fredric want with me that required such an unexpected display?

With a sigh, I set out across the street. As I neared, he

cracked his door. A long arm snaked out and beckoned, then when I was close enough, pulled me inside, slamming the door shut behind me.

"Help!" Fredric whimpered. "Lynley, you've got to help me!"

"What is it?" I stared around the tidy room and saw nothing out of place. My gaze returned to the young man with the red hair. Though his face was flushed and hapless, he was laughing.

"What?" I repeated.

Then I heard a sound from directly above me. Both Fredric and I looked up. There, on a blade of the ceiling fan, clung a kitten.

"*Mip*," said the kitten, followed by a big yawn.

"Help?" Fredric reiterated weakly.

I broke into a spontaneous grin. "Who do we have here?"

"That's Tarzan. They found him on the set of my new show. He was hanging around all by himself. Nobody else would step up, so I took him."

"How did he get up there?"

Fredric made bouncing motions with his hand, indicating the chair, the bookshelf, the curtain rod, and finally the fan itself. I understood.

"How old is he? Three months?" Fredric nodded. "Well, good luck. You have another year of this to look forward to before he turns into a cat."

Tarzan gave a further pathetic *mip*, then with legs spread like a flying squirrel, he launched himself into the air. Landing somewhat clumsily on Fredric's head, he dug in with his claws.

Fredric pulled him free and held him in his arms. "Youch, you little rascal!" Both man and kit blinked innocently at me. "Lynley, what am I going to do?"

I reached out and petted the baby fur, soft as a cotton ball. The gray tabby stripes would darken and solidify as he grew older, but for now, he more resembled a cloud of silver fluff.

"Are you going to keep him?"

"Yes, sure," Fredric replied without hesitation, then added, "If I can. I'm gone a lot working, sometimes overnight. I'll have to figure that part out. But yeah, he's my new wingman." Fredric looked lovingly at the little tabby face. "He's really smart. He can do tricks. Want to see?"

Before I could answer, Fredric moved to the table and placed the small body upon it. He turned, took a step, then turned again and tapped his collar bone.

"Tarzan, up!"

The puss crouched low, wiggled his behind, and took a flying leap onto the young man's shoulder where he twisted and settled into a mini loaf by Fredric's ear.

"Cool, eh?" He gazed around the room. "But his smarts gets him in trouble. I really need to kitten-proof this place."

"Has he been to the vet?" I grilled, ever the practical matron when it came to cat care.

"First thing—you've taught me that much. He got the works—flea meds, de-wormer, shots, and a checkup. Doc said he could stand to gain some weight but otherwise he's fine."

"Neutered?"

"He goes in Wednesday. But then what? I don't dare leave him alone here. I've been putting him in a dog crate I borrowed from the vet, but that isn't a solution."

"Friends of Felines gives an online class on kitten care.

I'd start with that. The fact is, I'm no expert. I work with cats on the other end of the progression—the old guys. But you seem to be off to a good start." I petted the fluffball again for which I received a soft bite with tiny but needle-sharp teeth. "Goodbye, Tarzan. Don't drive your dad too crazy."

Fredric held onto the kitten while I slipped out the door. He would have his hands full with that one!

As I cut across the street once more, I paused to gaze at my house, a turn of the century Old Portland holdover that I'd purchased before property prices skyrocketed in the early nineties. Aside from a tipsy shingle on the front porch roof and a bit of flaking paint, the place was in good shape for its age. It never ceased to amaze me how fortunate I was to have such a wonderful home.

Through my front window, I spied Emilio sitting on the sill. With his long, darker-than-dark fur, he resembled a fuzzy black hole. Big Red and another black floof, Tinkerbelle, were lying on the back of the loveseat. My eye shifted upward to find Little, the third of the black trio, peering down from one bedroom window while Hermione looked on from the other. I waved at them, suddenly thankful they were all sedate, polite, and fully-grown cats.

I still had some time before I needed to be at Darla's, so I decided to have a late lunch and catch up on my social media. I may have been past the big six-oh, but I had 1K Facebook friends who I was certain were just waiting to see what crazy cat story I would post next.

Pulling out a premade vegan rice bowl, I warmed it in the microwave. Several cats thought my presence in the kitchen meant it was time for them to eat too. I passed out cat-appropriate snacks while my bowl heated, so by the time the bell dinged, they were distracted enough to leave me alone.

I'd set the alarm on my phone for three o'clock in case I lost track of the time, which in truth, I did. There was an article on the Hawthorne All-Hallows Holiday Festival on one of the news channels, and I was deep into perusing the list of vendors when a bar of the original *Star Trek* theme brought me from my musings. In a way, I was relieved. Though it was fun to look at all the unique items, I preferred to do my shopping in person and would wait to decide what I wanted to buy till I got to the fête.

Shutting off the alarm and shoving the phone into my tote, I tried to think what I might need for the job. Nothing really—I'd only be there for a few hours, and if I did forget something important, I could always run home since it was just around the block. Still, it felt like a further journey, a journey into the unknown, and I needed to be prepared.

A shiver ran up my backbone and settled in the base of my neck, morphing into a slight headache. New things made me anxious—I knew that and did them anyway. Once I got to the house and settled in with the cats, the anxiety would abate. At least, that's what I told myself.

I put on my coat and tucked a hat in my tote in case it was raining when I returned. I thought about taking an umbrella, but being a staunch Portlander, I doubted I'd use it even if it poured. Umbrellas were for outlanders—people who moved here from California or Florida. The natives grew up spurning the useful accessory, preferring to get soaked and then complain about it. I'd never even owned an umbrella until someone gave me a lovely cat-print one. I used it occasionally, but more as a fashion statement than a way to stay dry.

The two-block stroll was bracing, and again I felt a

burst of excitement as I walked up the path to the house. I could see three cats in the catio in spite of the cool weather. They raised furry heads to check out who was coming into their territory but didn't leave their perches.

I let myself in with the key Darla had given me, then stopped in the small entrance way to get my bearings. It was only a little after four but already starting to get dark—inside the unlit house, it seemed pitch black. I felt the wall for a switch, found one, and flipped it. Surprisingly, instead of a single overhead unit, a half-dozen table lamps and wall sconces sprang to life. The effect was a gentle glow that fit perfectly with the ultra-minimalist décor.

"Well, kitties," I said as I took off my coat and hung it on a wrought iron contraption that I hoped was a coat rack and not a priceless piece of art. "How is the cat world? Are you hungry? Did your person leave you food like she said she would?"

Several pairs of eyes followed me as I bantered away, but only one came forward to greet me—Oscar, the dusky boy who reminded me so much of my own Emilio. As I bent down to pet him, I noted one difference—Oscar had two white toes!

"What now, sweetie? What do you cats like to do on a gloomy afternoon?"

I received no answer, nor did I expect one. When it came to social activities, I was on my own.

I began by making a tour of the room, checking the floor for any mishaps and saying hello to each cat individually. They were friendly for the most part, though some more than others. None besides Oscar were particularly interested in my presence. *How different from my own clowder*, I ruminated. At home, the cats would have been dogging my every step.

My first tour didn't turn up old Gloria, and I was beginning to worry when I discovered her sleeping in a cubby by the heater vent. I gave her a gentle pet to which she responded with a tiny purrumph, and then I let her be.

Working my way around to the dining table, I found a chartreuse envelope marked "Lynley" leaning against one of the cat beds. Beside it was a stack of photographs of the cats. I shuffled through those first, uttering a sigh of relief. Names and pertinent data had been penned on the back. They would be a huge help when it came to figuring out who was who.

I picked up the envelope and prized open the flap. Inside was a note that said only, "Please come again tomorrow." Stunned, I pulled out three crisp hundred-dollar bills. It seemed like a lot for two two-hour jobs, but then I didn't know the going rate for a cat sitter. If that was the pay, cat sitting might well be my new career!

I tucked the money back in the envelope and left both it and the photos on the table. Making my way into the kitchen area, I checked the automatic feeders which were packed to the brim with kibble, then went to the bubbler to make sure it was full as well—it was. I inspected the robotic litter box, an egg-shaped enclosure with a step tray and a night light in front of the oval door. Peeking inside, I saw it had been doing its job since the wheat-colored pellets were pristine clean. At first, I wondered how so many cats got along with just one commode, but then I saw a second machine set up in the corner of the living room and a third in the small front hall that I must have passed right by on my way in. Those were pricey items—it seemed Darla spared no expense when it came to her crew.

For a while, I sat at the table and studied the photos,

trying to memorize the names. Then I took a second tour of the room to match the felines with their pictures. Since it seemed my only real duty was to hang out with the cats, I located their toy box, found a long wand with ribbons, and tried to entice some play. Timmy and Tommy took the bait, as did the small brownish female Freyja, but the rest remained stubbornly on their beds and perches. Reluctant to indulge the stranger in their midst or just lazy cats? I did not yet know.

Finally, my select entourage tired of the game and sank to their bellies, content to watch the ribbons fly. I put the wand away, grabbed a rattle ball and a few catnip mice and tossed them in the middle of the floor.

"There you go, guys. You've tired me out and I need a rest. Everyone's welcome to join me."

I pulled a book from my tote, plopped myself down on the couch, and began to read.

* * *

An hour later, I had two cats on my lap and another two beside me on the sofa. Several more had stopped by for a visit, then gone about their business of sleeping and eating. As I listened to them crunch at the food stations and lap at the water fountain, I got to wondering how, with the automatic machines, Darla measured their intake. How could she tell when one was eating too much or another not enough? Watching a cat's eating habits was an important factor in judging their wellbeing, since loss of appetite may signify an illness. Again, I had the feeling that Darla was not as cat-savvy as one would expect of someone with so many cats. Still, it was none of my business. The cats seemed healthy and happy so who was I to judge?

My alarm pinged five o'clock—my first cat-sitting experience was coming to an end. I was ready and frankly a bit antsy to get home where I could do something besides read and scroll through my phone. Tomorrow I'd bring my crocheting and maybe my red sketchbook to play with in between petting the cats.

I was about to take off when I heard the classic *brrring* of a telephone. Shifting Oscar to the couch, I rose and followed the sound to a glass-faced cabinet. Sure enough, inside squatted an old fashioned landline model, brown with push buttons. I'd noticed it before but assumed it was an artifact, never guessing it might still be hooked up and functional.

Next to the phone sat a boxy answering machine of equal vintage. As the ringing stopped, the machine clicked on, and I heard Darla's voice give a brief message.

I was about to go back to my cat couch, when a new voice came on the line, a man I concluded, though he was either whispering or terribly hoarse.

"Dee," he hissed. "It's Mickey. I've got the drugs. Call me as soon as you can. If you don't want 'em, I know others who do."

Chapter 6

Do your cats appear in your dreams? Dreaming of a cat who has crossed the Bridge can feel like a precious visit, while a dream of your cat becoming lost is a nightmare.

The ambiguous message I'd overheard on Darla's archaic answering machine haunted me. I thought about it when I got home as I made dinner and fed the cats. I thought about it while trying to go to sleep. I even dreamed about it—a fantastical scenario involving dancing kittens, a Gotham-like city, and vampires though they may have been fairies. By the time I woke up next morning, I was sick of thinking about it, so I made a point of concentrating on other things such as putting in my volunteer shift at the shelter. But even that didn't succeed in distracting me, and next thing I knew, I was seeking out my best friend and tell-all buddy Frannie DeSoto. If anyone could make sense of my predicament, it was the level-headed Frannie.

Frannie and I had clicked from our very first meeting as new volunteers so many years before. The friendship grew, and now I couldn't imagine my life without her. To look at us, we were an unlikely pair—she with her pristine attire and impeccable makeup, and me more of an aging hippie type with few nods to face paint and dress. Still, as the saying goes, it's what's in a person's heart that matters. The older I got, the more that rang true.

We arranged to meet in the break room when Frannie finished her job stuffing envelopes for the shelter's upcoming fundraiser. I'd poured two cups of coffee from the coffee maker and grabbed a table by the window when she walked in. There was the usual smattering of small talk—*how are you, how are the cats,* etcetera—then we got down to business.

"So just as I was about to go home," I was saying, "the phone rang, and someone said—in a very suspicious voice, I might add—'I got the drugs.' "

Frannie pushed a platinum curl out of her face, then furrowed her painted brows. "You answered her cell phone? She didn't take it with her?"

"Not a cell—a landline. With an answering machine like the ones we had back in the olden days. When it came on, I couldn't help but hear every word."

Frannie pulled a plaid linen napkin out of her bag, followed by a green apple and a granola bar. "You don't mind if I lunch while we're talking, do you?"

"No, go ahead. I know you're busy with the fundraiser. I'm just glad you had time to meet."

"Always time for my bestie." Frannie unwrapped the granola bar, one of the soft, expensive kind with lots of dark chocolate chips in it, and took a bite. "'I have the drugs,' " she mused as she munched.

"No, it was—" I lowered my voice and hissed, " 'I *got* the drugs.' Colloquial English, like a dealer might use."

She shook her head, sending that mop of permed tresses bouncing. "That doesn't make any sense. Why would a drug dealer phone someone on their landline and leave a message that anyone could overhear?"

"I don't know. I don't think they would. But what else could it be? He called her by name—well, by a nickname— so it wasn't a wrong number."

"A prank?"

"I suppose it could have been." I sipped my coffee distractedly. "But that raises a different set of questions, such as why would someone be pranking Darla, and if they are, does it suggest the possibility of danger?"

"Danger?" Frannie replied. "What sort of danger?"

"I don't know. I enjoy a joke from time to time, and I appreciate the practical kind may be humorous to some, but there's the other side of it as well. Some people taunt others, harass them. Even stalk. You don't suppose Darla has a malicious stalker, do you?"

"No, of course not. What are you thinking?"

I turned away, embarrassed by my flight of dark fancy. "Forget about it."

But I didn't take my own advice. I couldn't forget. This new thought had slithered into my mind, right up next to the peculiar answering machine message, and stuck.

"Maybe cat sitting for a stranger isn't such a great idea for you, Lynley," Frannie said pensively.

"I was only thinking of the cats when I took the job. I really hadn't considered that I'd be dealing with people as well."

"How long do you have to go before she comes home?"

I took another sip of coffee. The bitter black taste stirred my senses even more. "Just tonight."

"Can you call her and tell her something came up?"

"Not really. She's off on vacation—how would she find another sitter at this point? No, I made the commitment and I'll see it through."

Frannie gave me the eye but said nothing.

"It should be fine," I added. "Weird phone calls aside, everything's gone smoothly so far. The cats are sweet and well-behaved. Besides, she's already paid me. Three-hundred dollars—in cash."

Frannie made a whistling sound. "Wow! Really? Now, that I do find suspicious."

I was taken aback by her reaction. "What? Why?"

"Lynley, that's a lot! Way a lot! My neighbor is a professional pet sitter. She sits for several people in my building. She charges twenty-five dollars for a two-hour visit and only fifty for an entire overnight."

"Really? I had no idea. I don't go out of town much, and with Seleia always up for a sleepover, I haven't had to hire a sitter for years."

I paused, thinking. "You know, there's something else that's strange about this job. Well, not about the job itself, but about the house. Darla has a back room that she expressly told me to stay out of. There's even a sign on the door."

"Her bedroom? Maybe she's a very private person. Or has some foibles she doesn't want you to know about."

"No, I don't think so."

Frannie had gone back to concentrating on her lunch. "Then what?" she posed before chomping into her apple.

"I don't know, and that's the problem. You know how I am with mysteries."

Frannie wiped her mouth with the napkin, then said in a mock-menacing voice, "Maybe that's where she stores the drugs."

I forced a laugh. "I'm making too much of it, aren't I? People have their quirks, and it's understandable there would be places in a home you wouldn't want your cat sitter to go. I'm blowing this all out of proportion, aren't I?"

"Maybe a little. It's good to trust your instincts, but don't let yourself get carried away. Not everything has evil intentions."

"Of course not," I affirmed self-consciously.

Frannie frowned and touched my hand. "Would you like me to call you later, just in case?"

I stared in surprise. All humor had fled from her face, and she was serious as stone.

Rising, I went to the sink where I rinsed out my coffee cup and put it in the dishwasher. Returning to the table, I picked up my purse, then paused.

"Yeah," I said thoughtfully. "If you don't mind, I'd like that very much."

Chapter 7

Cats need to play in order to be happy and fulfilled. Play time for them mimics the hunt of their wildcat ancestors.

Some hours later, settled on Darla's couch with Gloria on my lap, I'd forgotten all my misapprehension. Comfy in the quiet little house, surrounded by napping cats, I couldn't imagine having a care in the world.

As the twilight came on, shadows crept into the room like ghosts, but friendly ones. I hadn't noticed on my first visit, so eager had I been to banish the dark, but the place was strung with tiny fairy lights that glimmered like fireflies. They gave off just enough glow for my dark-adapted eyes to see things around me, but not so much as to distinguish what those things were. The circular shape was the table, and the lumps on top of it the cat's beds, but what was that pyramid? I easily distinguished the familiar form of cats along the window ledge by their rounded features, though the one on the end was too big even to be Oscar—it must have been a pillow.

I thought about turning on a light but hesitated. There seemed no need to disturb the magical ambiance. Besides, I couldn't displace Gloria who was sleeping so soundly, at least not yet.

A muffled buzz echoed from the back of the couch: my phone. I'd been reading an article on kitten care—a nod to Fredric and his new wingman—but I'd put it aside, and it must have slipped down between the cushions because now I could see it glimmering away against the white fabric.

"Frannie!"

"Hi, Lynley," came my friend's familiar voice. "This is your check-in call, making sure you haven't been kidnapped by drug dealers."

"No dealers," I sighed, "nor anyone else, for that matter. All quiet here if you don't count a few cat snores. Gloria is on my lap."

"The old blind one? How lovely. Well, I just wanted to make sure you were okay. You seemed concerned about that weird phone call when we talked today."

"Maybe not so much concerned as curious. I think it comes from being alone in a stranger's house. But everything's fine. I don't know why it got to me."

"Best to be cautious when you're off somewhere by yourself," Frannie comforted. "And I don't mind being your check point."

"I appreciate that. I'm going to stay here a bit longer, maybe try to get some of these guys to play." I glanced around at the sleeping shadows. "Though they look pretty comfortable where they are now."

"I'll let you go then."

"Okay. Thanks for calling." I hesitated. "And thanks for being a friend."

"Back at you," Frannie said before she clicked off the line.

Gloria had decided sometime during the phone call that my lap was no longer quite as restful as she wished it to be. She stood, stretched, and slipped down to the floor. I watched her, entranced by the efficient way she navigated the room despite her disability. With total confidence, she made for the feeder where she hunkered down to munch a snack. If one didn't look at her face, one would never guess she couldn't see what she was doing.

I rose and wandered the room, searching out toys the cats had distributed across the floor. Catnip mice, kicker pillows, sparkly balls, all looking like they just came out of the package.

I found the ribbon wand shoved under a chair and began to shake it, setting its little bells to tinkling.

"Okay, guys. Time for some exercise. You can't just lie around all day."

A couple of furry heads rose at the invitation, but no one jumped up to answer the call. I spent a few more minutes flicking the ribbons seductively along the sleeping ledge and was rewarded with a bat or two, but they lacked enthusiasm. I felt a stab of concern. Cats needed to play. It was hardwired into their routine, replacing the hunting instinct with something tamer. Cats who didn't play were either depressed or ill. But they'd played the day before, so this was probably a timing thing. I'd have to schedule my subsequent visits not to coincide with their afternoon nap.

Will there be more visits? I suddenly wondered. I'd told Frannie this would be the last one; now I couldn't remember why I'd felt so reticent. It was easy money, and I'd bonded with a few of the crew. Of course I'd come back if Darla asked me.

I tucked the wand back in the toy box and went to the kitchen area for a drink of water. As I stood by the farmhouse sink, I thought I heard a thump. Quickly I turned off the faucet, then stood stock still to see if the sound came again. Sure enough, after a moment there was another knock.

I tried to discern its origin. A windblown branch hitting the side of the house? A car door from down the street? But the next bump seemed closer, more like it was inside, not out.

The sounds were soft, so soft I wondered if I had heard them at all. I would have been happy to chalk it up to my imagination except it kept happening.

I turned and moved as silently as possible into the middle of the kitchen, then listened again. It was coming from down the hall.

The weak glow from the fairy lights made little headway into that cave-like hallway. Even so, I stared at the dark, willing my eyes to give me a clue. The sounds hadn't seemed threatening—I just wanted to know what they were so I could get back to being cozy with cats.

The house was utterly still now, and again I wondered if I'd been deceived by noises echoing in from somewhere else. I was about to turn away, turn back to the comfort of the light when it came one more time, accompanied by another sound—a sigh.

No, my mind told me vehemently. *No, that wasn't a sigh, at least not a human one. There weren't any humans holed up in Darla's bedrooms. Unless…*

The locked room! Who knew what she had stashed away in there? Something she didn't want anyone to see, that was for certain.

Any normal person would have walked away at that point. But not me. I wanted… *needed* to solve the mystery or there would be no peace.

I moved to the mouth of the hallway and stood a moment longer. Then, not being totally bereft of my senses, I found the switch and clicked on the overhead light.

Everything looked the same as it had when Darla took me on my brief tour. The bathroom, the bedrooms to the right and left, and the blue door with its portentous signage at the far end.

So far so good, I muttered to myself as I began tiptoeing down the hall. I kept my ears tuned, but whatever was thumping and sighing had gone silent. I glanced in the door on the right—Darla's small bedroom. Nothing awry there. The left-side room was a guest room. I could make out a single bed stacked with folded laundry or possibly bolts of fabric, since there was a sewing machine on a bench nearby. I'd nearly made it past when I caught the flicker of movement. Without thinking, I detoured into the doorway and turned on the light.

Shadows that had seemed threatening in the dark melted into ordinary things one would find in the spare room of a creative person—a dresser piled with craft items; a card table stacked with pots of beads. The space was cluttered and in disarray, but no more than would be natural for a workroom. As I spied several lengths of colored tulle, I pictured the skirt Darla was wearing at our meeting. She must have made it herself.

Then I noticed something else. Over the window hung a set of wooden blinds. They were closed, their honeyed color giving a soft feel to the room. One of the pulls, a long braided string with a large mahogany bead on the end hung directly over the heater vent. As the furnace blew warmth into the air, the bead swung back and forth, hitting against the wall. It was doing that now—clack, clack, clack.

Then the furnace shut off, and the movement stopped abruptly. The bead hung motionless, as it would until the heat blew on again. With relief, I turned away, clicked off the light, and returned to the quiet living room, my curiosity appeased.

Gloria was waiting for me on the couch, beckoning me to be her lap cushion again, and now that I'd traced down the mysterious thump, I was happy to comply. Seems I'd made an unconscious decision to forget all about the inexplicable sigh.

Chapter 8

By slowly introducing a new cat into your cat family, you can avoid stress and the possibility of a bad relationship. Both the new addition and the resident cats need time to become accustomed to each other.

I went back to reading the kitten article, but my heart wasn't into it. The incident of the enigmatic thump that had turned out to be nothing more than the clack of a blind pull had given me a scare, and contrary to instinct, being scared puts me right to sleep. Gloria was on the cushion beside me purring, or maybe it was snoring. Either way, the rhythm was hypnotic. Every so often, the litterbox hummed as it did its automatic cleanse. The water fountain burbled softly, and sometimes I'd hear the lap of a cat drinking there. Cars rumbled past on the quiet neighborhood street, but they were few and far between. Once I heard the voices of walkers, a girl laughing, a man's murmur in low tones.

The soft lights, the soft sounds, the soft cats all conspired to lull me into a dreamlike state. I took off my glasses, closed my eyes, and let my head fall back on the pillow. Synchronizing my breathing with that of the cats, I drifted into sleep.

In my dream, I heard the rattling of chains. I was in a basement—no, a dungeon. The chains were wound in circlets that hung from the stone walls like wreaths. Then they were wreaths, festoons of wheat and laurel strung with lights as if for some pagan holiday. The rattling sound had become the ringing of bells, and the dungeon, a grand hall with an open ceiling, stars twinkling above.

I blinked my eyes. The stars were still there. I blinked again, bringing the fairy lights into focus. Then I remembered where I was, the Cat House, sitting Darla's cats.

Gloria was still with me—how long had I been asleep? But another question popped into my mind: what was it that had woken me?

I went to sit up, then thought better of it. Something was off in the room—I could feel it. Something was different. It smelled of the outdoors, wet leaves and loam. That's when I noticed a black shadowy shape hovering by the entranceway.

This time I did sit up, adrenaline forcing me out of my stupor. Grabbing for my glasses, I stared at the dour shape, watching for movement, but it remained still as death.

Realizing it was only the sculpted coat tree, I began to relax, but the feeling was fleeting. It couldn't have been my coat—this shape was bigger, longer, darker, and more than a little ominous in the half-light.

As I panned the room for anything else out of order, I heard it, someone shuffling around in the kitchen. A drawer opened, and I made out the clattering of knives.

"Drat!" someone exclaimed, then the drawer slammed shut. A bumping and tumbling ensued, then the mew of a cat. "Drat!" the familiar voice repeated, this time with vehemence.

"Darla?" I ventured.

"I'm sorry, Lynley," the cat lady sighed. "And I was trying to be so quiet."

There was a click, and the kitchen light came on,

revealing the owner of the house bending down to right a gray plastic cat carrier that lay cattywampus on the floor. She was garbed far differently from our last encounter in a long black designer dress with a hood.

She pushed the hood back off her rainbow hair and smiled. "You looked so comfortable there with Gloria, I didn't want to disturb you."

I sat up, feeling awkward and self-conscious. "I'm sorry. I must have…"

"Don't apologize. I think cat sitters are allowed to nap. In fact, they are expected to, aren't they? It makes the cats feel safe."

"Oh, okay. I don't think I was very long…" I added, still feeling sheepish about being caught sleeping on the job, even if it was a sanctioned cat nap.

Darla hefted the carrier onto the kitchen counter. A louder mew ensued. This time I couldn't resist coming to investigate.

Peering through the grid of the carrier door, I was confronted by a wild yellow eye. "You got another one?"

"This is Newberry," Darla announced proudly. "She's a rescue, like the others. Her person became incapacitated and took her to a shelter where my friend works. When the shelter deemed the cat unadoptable, my friend called me and asked if I would give her a chance…" She stared fondly at the carrier, then up at me, all innocence and smiles. "How could I say no?"

Just then, Timmy, or maybe it was Tommy—I was still working to tell the tuxedo cats apart—jumped onto the counter to investigate.

"Look, Tommy," Darla said in the falsetto voice people use with their animals. "I brought you a new sister. Isn't she the cutest…?"

The two felines eyed each other briefly, then with a great hiss, Tommy lunged at the wire door. The newcomer shrank to the back of the carrier, but without the option of retreat, she was trapped. She gave a screech of warning which Tommy answered with his own wail.

As if it were a kitty call to arms, the kitchen was suddenly inundated with cats, all eager to see what was up. I looked to Darla for guidance—they were her cats after all, and she must have gone through the introduction process before—but all she did was throw up her hands in surrender.

The yowling got louder. Billy had joined Tommy on the counter, and now the both of them were pawing at the carrier gate. I peered through an air hole to see poor Newberry panting with fright, trying to hide underneath her own body since there was nothing else, not even a towel, let alone a bed pad, with which to conceal herself.

"She's hyperventilating!" I exclaimed, but Darla seemed stuck in place, her face a mask of surprise, and her red lips frozen in a perfect O.

"You have to get her out of here," I reiterated, then when there was still no response, I barked, "Darla! Look at me."

The woman's gaze edged away from the cat spectacle. Her face had gone utterly blank. Then whispering, she pleaded, "What should I do?"

"You need to get this cat away from the rest of them until she has a chance to calm down. Take her into another room."

Darla continued to stare a moment longer, then she nodded vigorously. "My bedroom. We can put her there."

Without waiting, I grabbed the carrier and headed for the back hallway. Darla slipped in front of me to turn on the light. We ducked inside, and I set the carrier on the bed, a double trundle style shaped like a wooden boat.

"Close the door," I commanded. "Quickly, before the others come."

Darla, though seemingly unable to make decisions on her own, was prompt to follow my instructions. She shut the door softly, then turned to the new cat. Passing her hand across her forehead as if she'd done a great task, she sighed.

"It's never been this bad before, Lynley. I swear!" She shook her head. "The new cats? Oh, there's always a bit of posturing when they meet the crew, but they come around. I don't understand why this one is so different."

My mind reeled. Was she serious? Didn't she know you have to introduce a new pet slowly? How had this crazy cat woman missed one of the basic rules of cat care?

Since it didn't look like Darla was up for much more than standing aside and feeling sorry for herself, I turned to the cat. Sitting gently on the bed next to the carrier, I flipped the latch. Newberry glared at me from within the plastic cavern but made no move to come out. At least she was no longer panting.

Taking my own calming breath, I said to Darla, "All cats are different. Some are more territorial than others."

"But the crew, they all get along…" she persisted.

"And that's good," I encouraged, suddenly feeling like I was about to give a lecture. "You've been lucky so far. But it doesn't mean every cat is going to act the same way. Newberry is a new entity. If she's a timid cat, her own fear could be setting off a fear reaction in the others. Or there may be a triggering smell on her that Tommy doesn't like. He might just feel he needs to defend his environment from something he perceives as a threat. You won't know until you've had more time to watch their behavior. That's why it's so important to give cats a chance to become comfortable with each other before putting them together."

The young woman came to sit beside me, peering into the carrier with its unhappy resident. She made to reach inside but I stopped her.

"I wouldn't just yet. Let Newberry make the first move. Otherwise, she may feel intimidated."

Darla withdrew her hand. "You know so much about cats," she grumbled. "I wish I had half your savvy."

I wish you did too, I thought to myself without mercy, but held my tongue.

"Was Tommy one of your original cats?" I asked instead.

Darla nodded. "He and his brother were the first."

"That makes sense. He wants to make sure Newberry knows her place."

"So what do I do?"

I shrugged. "Well, first off, keep them separated. Keep Newberry in here with her own food, water, and litterbox until she's had time to adjust to the change. In a week or so, you can begin to let her meet the others, briefly and under your supervision with treats all around. Friends of Felines has a video on how to introduce a new cat. You should look it up."

I knew I was being bossy—Darla was my employer which made me the employee—but my patience was wearing thin. Questions raced through my mind like speeding cheetahs. Why would the woman get another cat? She already had enough to start her own rescue. And how had she come by this one? I thought she'd been on vacation. Most of all, I wondered why she knew so little about taking care of Newberry now that the cat was here?

Then a thought struck me. What if Darla really was a *crazy cat lady*? Or to use a harsher term, a hoarder?

"I've got to go," I said suddenly. "They're expecting me..."

But I didn't move. Instead, I looked once more at the poor scared cat in the carrier. Her eyes connected with mine and she extended a tentative paw. I touched it softly. She withdrew it again, but slowly.

"Will she be alright?" Darla queried.

"I think so. See, she's responding already. Just keep her away from the others. Spend time with her. Listen to what she tells you."

At that last, Darla gave me a questioning look but said nothing.

As I rose to leave, she caught my hand. "Thank you, Lynley. I don't... I just... I'm glad you were here."

"Watch that video," I said solemnly. "Do you need me to send you the link?"

"No, I can find it. I'm familiar with Friends of Felines shelter. And I'll watch it right away. I guess I have a lot to learn about cats."

I paused. "None of us ever stop learning."

We let ourselves out of the bedroom, making sure no one else snuck in, and Darla followed me to the front room where I picked up my things and shrugged on my coat.

"So I have another trip planned at the end of the week," she asserted. "I'll need you back then. Will that work for you?"

I was surprised, both at the quick turnaround of her *vacations* and the audacity of asking me to come back at all. I wasn't sure I ever wanted to work for her again, at least not until I figured out what was going on with her. If she really was a cat hoarder, I could be getting myself in over my head. Dealing with hoarders was a job for a humane investigator, not a cat sitter lady. A good plan would be to call my friend Special Agent Denny Paris and let him look into it. At the very least, I should discuss my concerns with him before making any commitments.

But then I caught sight of Gloria curled on the couch, pointing her face toward me as if she were watching. I walked back and gave her a lingering, loving pet.

"Let me know when you want me," I sighed, and then I left. With the onset of the new cat issue, I'd totally forgotten to ask Darla about the phone call… and about the drugs.

Chapter 9

Kittens enjoy warmth and closeness, but putting them in the pocket of your clothing can be overwhelming. Your movements may disorient them, and they cause them to feel trapped if the pocket is big and dark.

I was barely in my front door when I remembered I'd forgotten something. Many people in my sphere ordered their cat supplies online and had them conveniently delivered, but I still frequented a little local pet shop run by a single lady with a cat of her own. I'd spent more time at Darla's than planned, and after the kerfuffle with her new cat family member, the fact I needed to pick up my purchase of cat food and litter from the Pet Pantry had completely slipped my mind.

Though it was dark as midnight, in reality it was only a little after six, still an hour before the pet store closed for the evening. I quickly fed the cats, then grabbed my purse and ran for my car.

It was a fast trip in spite of the remnants of five-o'clock traffic, and I slipped into the shop to see Harlene up on a step ladder hanging what looked like Christmas decorations. She had swapped her usual peach-colored "Pet Pantry" apron for a smock of red and green trimmed with gold rickrack. With her round, squat figure, she could have been a Christmas ornament herself.

She turned at the tinkle of the entry bell, her face alight and her bright blue eyes shining.

"Lynley! I'd nearly given up on you. Your things are there." She nodded to a stack of items, several cartons of varying sizes as well as a small cat tree, set by the door. "I'll call Daniel to help you to your car just as soon as I get this one..." She grunted, reaching up to clip a garland to the picture rail. "This one..." she repeated, stretching farther and looking extremely unstable on the little ladder. "This one... darned... branch... Oh well," she sighed as she lost her grip, and the swag dangled to the ground. Peering at the rebellious decoration, she mumbled, "I rather fancy it that way."

Flouncing down off the step stool and shoving the remaining garland clips into one of her smock's voluminous pockets, she gave a sweeping gesture and smiled. "What do you think, Lynley? Isn't it magic?"

I surveyed the twinkle lights, the festive greenery, and the hanging garland which did actually look quite nice with its asymmetrical flounce. "It's lovely, but I think you've gotten ahead of yourself. It's not even Halloween yet."

"The early birdie gets the millet," she pronounced, veganizing the old proverb.

Moving to an easy chair, a set of two placed comfortably around a coffee table scattered with pet literature, she plopped down with an *oof*. No sooner had she landed than her shop cat Scout appeared out of nowhere and jumped on her lap to curl and purr.

"Did you know," she posed as she petted the pretty seal-colored feline with the deformed lip, "that shoppers are most likely to make impulse buys the very first time they encounter holiday décor? Doesn't matter if it's Thanksgiving, Halloween, or the Fourth of July—that first moment they see those sparkly reminders of the Christmas season, they get all warm and fuzzy and stricken with the desire to purchase gifts. By the time the season begins in earnest, they've been inundated with ads—buy this; buy that; if you really loved her, you'd buy her a car. It's all downhill from there."

"I see your point" I said, coming to sit in the other chair. "Though I'm not sure I approve. There's enough stress and pressure around Christmastime without needing to start months ahead."

"I understand, my friend, but you don't own an independent business. Times are tough. We do what we must to survive."

"Well, I promise to do all my holiday impulse pet buying here, if that helps. But not now, if you don't mind. I've still got a Halloween fête to get through before I can begin thinking about Christmas shopping."

"Oh?"

"My granddaughter's got herself involved in the new Hawthorne All-Hallows Holiday Festival."

"How fun! I've been hearing about that. I was thinking of getting a vendor space myself but never got around to putting in the application. Do you know if there are still openings?"

"I don't, but you might inquire. Since it's the first time they've done it, they're likely to have a few leftover spaces."

Harlene pulled her phone from her pocket, held it to her mouth and said, "Call All-Hallows about booth space." Clicking off, she replaced the instrument in her smock. "I find I've got to keep reminders these days. I don't know if my brain is too full to remember everything, or there's just a lot more to remember, but if I don't make a note, it flies away with the fairies."

Her hand had lingered in the pocket and now she withdrew a folded sheet of paper. "Speaking of reminders, here's your invoice. I got everything you wanted except the water fountain. It's on backorder—some supply chain issue. Who knew a locally-made ceramic burbler would have parts from China?"

"That's okay. I have one already, but I wanted a second for the foster cat room. I don't have any fosters right now so it can wait."

Harlene passed me the paper, and I opened it to find the long list of cat items I'd ordered. As I glanced down the list, I sat forward with a jolt, remembering something else I'd forgotten, or at least put to the back of my mind—Dirty Harry's birthday.

"I think I'm going to have to start leaving myself reminders too—I totally spaced on Harry's birthday party."

"Dear me. Poor neglected Harry. How old will he be?"

"Seventeen, though it's not his real birthday. I have no idea when he was born since he came to us as a stray. But the first week of November is when we found him and took him in. So this is more of an *adoptiversary*, I suppose."

"Seventeen!" Harlene exclaimed. "Not every cat achieves the grand old age of seventeen. Every day is to be celebrated."

"Some live a lot longer," I insisted.

Harlene reached over and touched my hand. "And I'm sure your Dirty Harry will be one of those."

We sat for a moment in silence, contemplating that thing every cat person fears the most, the decline of their feline companion. I noticed Harlene give Scout a little loving hug.

I stuffed the invoice in my purse and stood. "I'd better

be going. You're about to close up, and I need to get home."

"Of course. Let me get Daniel."

But instead of yelling the stock person's name, as she'd done on past visits, she once again retrieved her phone to text the young helper. It was a much quieter method but lacked the personality of a good Harlene yell.

It seemed to work just as fast though because Daniel was there in a heartbeat. A man-boy of about twenty with the lanky look of a teenager but a good set of muscles underneath his black tee shirt, he appeared from the back of the store with a smile on his face.

"Ah, Danny, can you help Ms. Cannon out to her car? Those are her things over by the door."

Daniel's smile grew wider, and he nodded enthusiastically as if he lived to do his employer's beckoning. Harlene had that effect on her assistants—I didn't know if it was just her embracing personality or if she bribed them with goodies in the break room.

Daniel went to inspect the order, eyeing the cat tree. "What kind of car do you have, Ms. Cannon?"

I came to stand beside him. "It's a Toyota. A little one. The cat tree might take some maneuvering, but the rest can fit in the front seat."

He scratched his head. "Let me take a look."

"You can probably fold down the back seat and pass it through from the trunk. Here are the keys."

Daniel loaded my items on a hand truck and rolled it out to my car. As I watched through the window, I felt a sudden sense of dread. Young men his age had been going missing—would this kind helpful boy be next?

Harlene joined me at the door. "You watch out for him, won't you?"

Harlene gave me a knowing look. "Always."

We said our goodbyes, and pushing my fears aside, I promised to return for my holiday shopping once it really was the holidays.

* * *

There is always an issue with buying something heavy or awkward—the people at the store are more than happy to cart it to one's car, but what does one do once home? Where was that muscular youth to wrangle the thing into the house? I usually get by, but not without effort and sometimes a backache the next day.

Most of the things from the pet store weren't that heavy—flats of cat cans, bags of kibble, and Harry's very special, locally made birthday present, already wrapped in cat print tissue paper and ready to go. The tubs of litter were a bit more of a challenge, but I hefted them onto the porch, one by one, without harming myself. There, they could sit until I had need for them or someone came along to cart them to their intended destinations by the commodes around the house. No, those things I did without pause. It was the new cat tree that was the conundrum.

The tree was an impulse buy but one I'd wanted for a long time. I didn't really need it—I already had two, one in the living room and one in the kitchen, but this was a special design I'd seen advertised on Harlene's bulletin board. Made by Cat Black, craftsman of clever cat climbers, this one was designed like a windblown beach pine with baskets on the branches. Its wide, slanting trunk was an easy climb for older cats like Harry, as well as ones with special needs like Elizabeth, my "wobbly" cat. Elizabeth's feline cerebellar hypoplasia wasn't terribly pronounced, but her compulsive shaking made it difficult for her to navigate uprights.

Elizabeth had come a long way from the skinny, scrawny, shy little cat she had been when I adopted her a little over a year before. In her time with me, she had overcome her traumatic kittenhood as a feral with a disability. She had no concept of her limitations, so I often found her trying to climb higher than she should. It would be nice to have a tree she could scale without worry.

I'd made it inside with the rest of the load and was trying to wrangle the huge tree out of the back of my car—a feat in itself—when I heard the squeak of a door across the street. Brushing a lock of hair away from my glasses, I glanced over to see Fredric standing on his little cement porch smiling at me.

"What have you got there?" he called over. "Looks like a giant, many-headed snake."

I straightened, a little out of breath. "It's a new cat tree. I don't suppose you could give me a hand getting the darned thing out…" I bent down and gave it another yank. "I don't know how Daniel got it in here, but it seems to be stuck."

"Cat tree, eh?" he said, coming down and crossing the street to stand beside me. "Maybe it's grown a few more limbs when you weren't looking."

"I think you're right. Here, if you can pull, I'll get in the back seat and push."

I paused, noting Fredric's chest had begun to wriggle. Fredric noticed it too and unzipped his hoodie a few inches. Out popped a tiny tabby head. Tarzan the kitten blinked his eyes and gave a profound *mip*.

I started in surprise. "Do you always carry your kitten in your shirt?"

"Not usually. We were having a rest when I saw you battling that snake—I mean tree. But he seems to like it there."

"Keep an eye on his body language," I said, clicking over to teacher mode. "Being carted around in someone's clothing can be scary for a little cat."

"I will. Be right back."

Fredric turned and jaunted across the street, holding his hand to his chest to support the kitten. A minute later he returned, looking lighter in the torso.

With a great deal of heaving, wrenching, cajoling, to say nothing about grunting and swearing, we managed to wrestle the odd-shaped item from my car. Then came the awkward haul onto my porch and the conniving of it through the front doorway. Thankfully I'd already planned where it was going to go—in the front room beside the window—and cleared a place. Ten minutes later there was a tree in my living room all ready for feline clientele.

"Can I get you some tea or coffee?" I offered. "It's the least I can do for coming to my rescue."

"I'd better get back to Tarzan, before he throws a kitten fit and disasterizes the house."

I nodded. "He is at that age, isn't he?"

"He's getting better," Fredric defended. "Or maybe it's just that he's already broken everything he could reach, and I've put away the rest."

"I totally understand. And thanks."

Fredric spun around and started away but then paused, his back to me. I couldn't see his face, but all of a sudden, I had the feeling something was wrong. When he turned his head, I saw his look of despair.

"You got a minute, Lynley? I think I need help."

Chapter 10

Start your kitten traveling at an early age. Get them accustomed to a harness and leash or a stroller, and most important of all, their carrier.

"Maybe you'd like that coffee after all," I said to Fredric, who was standing like a statue of grief in my front hallway.

For a moment, he just stared at me. "Uh, yeah, maybe I would."

He glanced over at his duplex. I knew he was worried about leaving his kitten alone.

"Go ahead and collect Tarzan while I make the coffee."

"He won't bother your cats?"

I glanced into the living room where the clowder was gathered around the new cat tree. "I don't think so. They seem to be busy with their new toy."

"Thanks, Lynley." Fredric paused a moment longer, then left to retrieve his cat.

As I went to make the refreshments—black Colombian coffee for Fredric and a mug of Genmaicha for me—I couldn't help but wonder what was getting the young man down. I'd rarely seen him out of sorts—he was one to keep a level head in times of trouble. Something about the kitten? I didn't think so—it seemed more emotional than that. About his job? He'd recently been promoted to a full-fledged production assistant—had something gone wrong? But the look on his face was not that of someone with a work problem. That left Seleia. Last time I saw them together they'd seemed happy as ever, but things could happen fast at that age. I may be into my seventh decade, but I could still vividly recall the sting of first loves.

I heard the front door open and close. "We're back."

"Come on to the kitchen," I returned. "We can shut the door and give Tarzan the run of the place while we have our drinks."

Fredric complied, softly closing the kitchen door behind him before pulling the kitten out of his hoodie. Tarzan looked around, then gave a mighty squirm.

"You can put him on the floor. There's nothing for him to get into here."

Once free, the kitten wasted no time scampering from food station to food station. Since I'd already picked up the dishes, all he found was scent and disappointment.

"Is he hungry?" I asked needlessly—the only time kittens aren't hungry is when they're asleep.

"Probably. I need to get to the store soon for a restocking. I had no idea how much that little thing could eat."

"I think I have some kitten food stashed somewhere…"

I went to a cupboard filled with cans of various cat foods, picked through the collection, and pulled out a stack of small pink tins. "I got these for a kitten I was fostering several months ago. You're welcome to them."

Flipping open the top of the can, I took a whiff of the delicate meaty scent—not unappetizing, even to a vegan. I spooned half the contents into a small, flat bowl and went to place it on the floor. Tarzan was on it before I'd even set it down.

I brought the mugs of coffee and tea over to my dining table, a round, mission oak antique I inherited from my grandmother, and placed the coffee on a woven mat. "Come, sit."

The young man was sheepish about it. He sat, but only on the edge of the old chair. He took the handle of the mug but did not drink. His face was a mask, a not-quite-right smile obscuring something deeper that was nothing like a smile at all.

"You want to tell me what's bothering you?"

With eyes awash with sadness, he gave me a profound stare. "I think there's something wrong with Seleia."

My heart clenched. Something amiss with my precious granddaughter? Those are words no grandmother wants to hear.

Before the images of catastrophe and cataclysm could run rampant in my mind, I pressed, "What sort of wrong? Physical? Mental? Other?"

"We had a fight," Fredric said dourly.

I started to sigh with relief, fights between young couples being well into the normal range of things, but stifled it so Fredric wouldn't feel I was belittling his woe. He didn't seem to notice because he went on without interruption.

"I guess it was my fault. I was pushing her. But we've been together for a while now. I thought our relationship had grown stronger, that she wouldn't still be holding back…"

Oh! My! Gosh! I was instantly back on high alert. Were we talking about what I thought we were talking about? Was this man trying to push my innocent baby into *s. e. x.*?

Fredric totally missed my reaction, continuing to yammer about relationships and intimacy and things I didn't want to hear.

"…I know how seductive it can be," he was saying. "I

felt that pull myself when I first started."

I snapped back to the present conversation, realizing I'd missed something. "It? What *it*?"

"Acting, of course. What did you think I was talking about?"

"Oh, acting, of course. Sorry. Please go on."

"Seleia's completely swept up in it. Did she tell you she's thinking of changing her college major?"

"She mentioned it," I nodded.

"Acting is great—a true calling, and Seleia has talent, though it's still pretty raw at this point. But it's a hard road to travel. Hard to succeed among all the other wannabes, hard to even make a living. And it can be dangerous, especially for a beautiful young woman like Seleia. I'm not saying she's naïve, but there are bad people out there, people who... Well, I'd rather not spell it out, but you get the idea."

I did get the idea.

"Do you think Seleia is that serious about it? Taking drama in college isn't the same as running away to Hollywood."

Fredric sighed. "No, I suppose not. I just wanted her to fully understand what she's getting herself into."

"And you fought about it?"

"She thought I was telling her what to do. I wasn't. At least not really."

Tarzan had finished his meal and hunted down the litterbox where he was having a great time flinging litter every which way. We both watched the little cat as he hopped out and zoomed to Fredric. With a *mip*, he clawed his way up the young man's leg and settled onto his lap.

"I'll talk to her," I said. "I won't mention you," I added when Fredric looked up in fear. "I'm her grandmother. It's my job to tackle the hard questions. And to be honest, I've thought about it myself. It is a big change from astrophysics. She needs to think it through, maybe put off the switch until next year. That would give her time to consider."

Fredric brightened noticeably. "That might work. She could do some summer stock and get a little more experience under her belt before deciding. Every production is different. It could teach her a lot."

"This is her first try at acting. She may come to the conclusion it's not so exciting after all. Or she may find it's her life's calling. It's her choice. I know you want what's best for her, but that's something she has to decide for herself. Debate with her, and you'll just lose."

"But..."

"Look, I understand that you know the industry far better than she does, and I'm not trying to dissuade you from guiding her when you can, but you must know telling a woman what to do is a recipe for disaster. And telling a Mackay," I added, intentionally using our Scottish ancestral family name, "is even worse. Do that and you'll have her signing up for a ten-city tour of *Streetcar Named Desire* before you know it."

Fredric laughed. "She would make a great Stella, wouldn't she?"

"If she set her mind to it, I'm sure she would."

I watched Fredric pet his little cat who was now curled into a ball fast asleep. His smile had evaporated, and he was back to looking glum.

"Let her be herself," I encouraged. "She'll come around."

"I hope so," Fredric ruminated. "But it's not just that. Lynley, I'm worried. Seleia's changed."

* * *

A pensive Fredric departed by the back door, little Tarzan tucked into his jacket to keep him from the rain that had started to pour. A few moments later, I heard my front doorbell ring. Fredric returning for something forgotten? I didn't think so. If it were Fredric, he'd more likely have come back to the door through which he left.

I glanced up at the Kit-Cat clock on the kitchen wall. The vintage instrument with its swinging tail and roving eyes read eight-twenty, a bit later than most of my unannounced visitors. With a little flutter of apprehension, I went to see.

As I stepped into the hallway, I heard a familiar tap-tap—not Fredric but Seleia. Sure enough, there she was, huddled on the porch looking dismal. Behind her, the rain was pelting down like bullets.

"It's not locked," I called.

She wasted no time pushing inside. "Whew, Grandmother! What a downpour! It was so nice a little while ago I decided to walk."

I stared out at the rain, then shut the door against it.

"The storm only began a few minutes ago." She glanced through the window with a black look. "But it's making up for lost time."

"Well, you're out of it now, love. Come on in and I'll make you something to drink. Tea? Hot apple cider?"

She stomped her wet feet on the mat, then stripped off her coat and boots. "That would be splendid! Absolutely divine!"

Splendid? Divine? When did my granddaughter start using such words in everyday conversation?

Following me into the kitchen, she pulled out a chair from the oak table and flopped into it. Her eye instantly landed on the two mugs, still warm from their previous drinkers.

She looked at me coyly. "I see you've had a visitor, Grandmother. Anyone special?"

"Just a friend," I hemmed. I'm not sure why I didn't want to tell her it was Fredric. Still, if I were to pursue the issue of her newly chosen acting career, it was probably best not to involve even the slightest mention of the talk with the boyfriend—for his sake and for mine.

Retrieving a jar of fresh-pressed cider from the refrigerator, I poured it into a pan. "How are the rehearsals coming?" I asked innocently as I set the liquid to heat on the stove.

"Very well! It's going to be a wonderful performance. Of course there are still a few rough spots, but that's to be expected."

From there she lit into a mini-rant about actors who didn't come on time, extras who couldn't keep their places, and a man playing a lead who had bad breath. Listening only vaguely, I stirred a cinnamon stick and a few cloves into the heating juice, producing a heavenly scent of spice.

"Kiefer has me working day and night," Seleia sighed.

I looked around sharply, spoon suspended above the pan, and found that, despite the sigh, she was smiling.

"Kiefer?"

"Mr. Clark, our director."

Something about the way she said his name—a soft, gentle outbreath—made my grandmother senses tingle. Her face seconded what her voice betrayed—Seleia had a crush on her director!

It wasn't surprising. I'd looked up the fairly famous artist on the internet, where I was greeted by pages of mostly good press. According to his reviewers, Kiefer

Clark was a genius in his field. His headshot showed an attractive man in his early forties with just the hint of gray in his wayward dark hair and a few lines of wisdom giving character to the classic face. His eyes alone were enough to mesmerize someone of Seleia's age—wide and dark, reflecting the depths of his passions. As long as that passion was for the theater, I was all for it. If it even glimpsed the way of my granddaughter, I'd have something else to say.

But I was getting ahead of myself. Just because Seleia had a crush did by no means mean it was reciprocated. Still, I needed clarification on one detail.

"Working day and night," I repeated, pouring the steaming cider into a set of black cat Halloween mugs and placing them, along with a plate of cookies, on a tray. "Let's go in the living room and you can explain exactly what that means."

Seleia gave an embarrassed laugh as we repaired to the more comfortable quarters.

"Nothing," she flipped, taking her mug in her hands to warm them. "It means nothing. Just that we're working hard to make the best show we can. At least I am."

She settled into the sofa and took a sip of her beverage, sending the scent of apples through the room. I was silent, an unrevealing half-smile pasted on my face. I knew if I held the expression long enough, she would say more.

"It's not what you're thinking, Lynley," Seleia said, fulfilling my prophecy. "We're just friends."

Pause.

"I mean, he's way older than me."

Pause.

"And it wouldn't be right for an actor in a play to be involved with the director."

Pause.

"But it does happen. You read about it all the time."

Pause, this one for nearly a minute.

"Oh, Grandmother, I really do like him. He makes me feel… different, special. Like an adult instead of a gawky kid. Nothing's going on," she added quickly.

"But you wish it was?"

"Maybe. I don't know."

"And Mr. Clark," I said, intentionally using the older man's surname. "Does he know how you feel?"

Seleia gasped. "Of course not! He's always a perfect gentleman and treats me no differently than the rest of the cast. But sometimes I catch him looking at me."

I wasn't surprised at that statement. Seleia, with her beautiful auburn hair and radiant complexion, would turn anyone's head.

For a moment, the two of us were silent. My cats had embraced their new tree and were settled on the various perches. I watched Elizabeth toddle over, put her front paws against the slanted trunk, then scrabble her way into a low basket where she settled with a kitty sigh. As if she sensed my disquiet from across the room, she gave me a love blink, then tucked her head down into the plush and closed her eyes.

"What about Fredric? You two have been together for a long time."

"We had an argument," she admitted after some thought. "I feel like we're drifting away from each other. One part of me is devastated, but there's another part that wonders if a separation isn't inevitable."

"And why is that, dear?"

She turned to me, her brown eyes on the verge of tears. "He's changed, Grandmother. Fredric has changed."

Chapter 11

Many animal hoarders have the best of intentions, but the reality of caring for so many gets away from them, and they find themselves overwhelmed. These people are often willing to work with authorities for the good of their animals.

Seleia left for home, and I gathered up our dishes, as well as the mugs from Fredric's visit. Arranging them in the dishwasher, I set the machine to run. Then, with the quiet, oscillating hum of its cleaning cycle for background music, I sat down at the table to think.

Seleia and Fredric had been boyfriend and girlfriend for some years. He was her first beau—it was unlikely he would be her last. Still, there was something about the couple that seemed to defy the odds. They'd been good together, no matter what—until now.

Now it seemed both were harboring second thoughts. Seleia was bedazzled by an inaccessible older man, and Fredric was worried and probably a bit jealous. Each party accused the other of having changed. Change was inevitable, but that didn't mean it was easy.

Still, I reminded myself, like so many things in life, their relationship was none of my business. All I could do was to be there for Seleia if she needed me, and the same with Fredric, in the way of a friend.

Just then Mab zoomed into the room, followed at a more sedate pace by big Violet. Those two were best buds in spite of their differences, Mab being a sleek purebred lilac point Siamese *katten* whereas Violet was older, obese, and obstinate with everyone but Mab. The two played together, slept together, and would probably have eaten together if Violet weren't on a special diet.

I scooped Mab into my lap as she streaked by and watched Violet pull up short, wondering where her friend had gone. Mab snuggled into my shirt, and I petted her bunny-soft fur. Thank goodness for my furry family whose simple relationships centered on warmth, toys, and treats.

I jumped as my phone rang, launching Mab back to her game of chase with Violet. Checking the screen, I expected to find an unfamiliar number, spam from Missouri or Florida, but to my surprise, it showed a shiny gold badge icon with the name *Denny* beside it.

The Kit-Cat clock now read nine-thirty-five. Why was Humane Investigator Denny Paris calling me about at this late-ish hour? Since it was rare for him to call at all, it must have been important.

"Special Agent," I answered, enjoying the sound of his formal designation.

"Lynley Cannon," he shot back in a friendly tone, but even over the phone, I could hear his voice sober. "You got a minute?"

For you, always, I was about to quip but thought better of it. From his tone, this might not be a joking matter. "Of course, Denny. What's up?"

"I have a situation, and I think you could help. The Humane Investigations team received a call from some neighbors complaining that the cats belonging to the person next door weren't being properly fed and cared for. I've been to the property and met the owner, a fiftyish white woman named Judy Smith. She gave me permission to enter. It was pretty grim. She claims there are twenty-six cats, including a bunch of kittens. Between my own knowledge of the circumstances and the neighbors' statements, it's been decided that we take the cats into custody. As you can imagine, the owner isn't happy. That's where you come in."

"Me?" I'd helped the special agent in the past, so his request wasn't unprecedented, but as a cat shelter volunteer and not a professional, my assistance was limited.

"There are two ways this can go," he continued. "Either we convince Ms. Smith that relinquishing the cats is in everyone's best interest, or we remove the cats by force. We have a warrant, so everything's set and legal. I just need someone who can talk to her."

"Isn't that something you usually do?"

"She refuses to speak to a man or anyone in a uniform, so that makes me a double baddie, but you fit the bill perfectly. What do you think, Lynley? Will you do it?"

* * *

The next morning, way too early, I found myself sitting in the front seat of the Northwest Humane Society investigations truck. Denny was at the wheel, a careful, cautious driver whom I trusted with my life. So why did I feel like a cat headed for the veterinarian?

I glanced over at Denny, the handsome face, the curly sand-colored hair doing its best to escape the blue uniform cap. It always amazed me that he was an animal cop and not a film star. But vocation had more to do with soul than appearance, and his success at his job proved time and again he had chosen wisely.

The look in his cat-green eyes was pensive, as always when on a case. I knew he'd done his best to study the situation and account for all possibilities, but coming between people and their pets was unpredictable. What would we find when we got there? Would the owner be compliant, tearful, or holding a shotgun? We wouldn't know until we arrived.

"I can guess what happens if the owner refuses to hand over the cats, but what if she chooses to comply?"

"Lots of things," Denny replied. "Northwest Humane can provide education and assistance. We've got a social service who can come in and clean up the house. The case will go to an arbitrator. Depending on the outcome, it's possible a smaller number of cats may be returned to her, as long as she commits to not taking more in the future."

Then I thought of something else and decided to run with that. "I have a question for you on another subject—though it might be related in some ways."

He clicked on the signal for a left-hand turn. "Eh, what's that?"

"How many cats can a person have before they're considered a hoarder?"

Denny glanced over at me in surprise. "Why? Did someone accuse you of hoarding? Look, I know you have a lot of cats…"

"It's not me," I laughed, "though I understand why you might have jumped to that conclusion. No, I've been cat sitting for a woman in my neighborhood. She had nine cats when the job started; then yesterday she brought home another one, making it ten. She said someone asked her to take the cat, so she did. But thing is, she doesn't seem that cat-savvy. She had no idea how to introduce the new one, and there are other things, little things, that make me wonder what's up."

"You're cat sitting?" Denny remarked. "Since when?"

"This is my first time. It's sort of fun, but now that I've gotten to know the cats, I worry about them. The client's already got a houseful—why would she be bringing in more?"

He shrugged. "What compels you to adopt a new cat?"

That made me think. "Because they need me?"

"Sounds like she's doing the same."

"But I've had extensive training with cats. She didn't even know that most topical flea medications need to be applied monthly. And I always weigh the situation carefully before adding a new cat family member—she seems to be picking them up willy-nilly."

Denny frowned. "Are her cats well cared for—aside from the flea meds issue? Do they have enough food, water, clean litterboxes?"

"Yes to all that. She seems fastidious and very invested in their health. But I'm concerned because I don't think she knows what she's getting herself into."

Denny pulled up at a red light, then turned to me. "You worry too much, Lynley. It sounds like those cats have a good home—maybe not perfect, but certainly better than being on the streets or in a shelter. Still," he mused as he started through the green, "it can't hurt to keep an eye on her. You have good instincts. If she continues to bring home more cats, give me a call, and I'll come talk to her. She might just need some professional advice."

"Thanks, Denny. That makes sense. I do worry too much. But I really have become attached to some of her cats."

Denny listened indulgently as I went on about Gloria, Oscar, and the rest of Darla's crew. Before I knew it, we'd arrived at our destination.

Denny pulled up in front of the small stucco-fronted

house. Once low-cost dwellings, those nostalgic vintage homes now went for a pretty penny. Judy Smith must have had money at one time, though from the chipped paint and rotting window frames, it may not have been for a while. The little garden was a tangle of weeds and shrubbery gone wild. It didn't take money to prune your bushes—that sort of neglect spoke of an issue other than lack of funds.

Now that we were there, my apprehension resurged. What was I going to say to this woman who liked cats better than men? If someone came to take my cats away, I would also fight tooth and claw. But my cats weren't neglected. Maybe she merely needed help with food or cleaning. Maybe there was something we could do for her, short of removing the cats. Maybe I could persuade her that we weren't the enemy. Denny was counting on me, so I'd better be ready to try.

A van pulled up behind us, and a truck after that.

"NWHS is sending a videographer," Denny explained, "and trained volunteers to gather the cats. There's a state trooper to accompany them, just in case."

"In case of what?"

Denny bypassed the question. "Stay here, Lynley," he commanded as he went to meet the others of his team. I did as he bid but rolled down the window. He'd said nothing about not listening in.

Four men and two women gathered around the back of the vehicle. I recognized Denny's partner, Special Agent Connie Lee, but the others were strangers to me. After a round of greetings and introductions, Denny got right down to business.

"Okay, we don't know what we're up against here. The owner has been in compliance for the most part, but she became aggressive when I mentioned taking the cats away. Special Agent Lee will go first with the warrant and to explain what we're here to do. What happens next depends on how that goes."

I peered in the rearview mirror. Denny was shifting on his feet, a sure sign he anticipated a conflict.

"Conduct yourselves with decorum at all times," he went on. "No loud talking, laughing, cussing, or derogatory remarks. Damon will video all communications, as well as the animals and their situation once we get into the house. Try to give only factual observations and qualified comments as long as the tape is running."

There was a pause. I couldn't see enough to gauge what was going on. Then I heard my name.

"Ms. Smith has asked to speak to a woman not affiliated with the police force, and I have Lynley Cannon standing by. Lynley is a long-time volunteer with Friends of Felines and a cat expert. She's good with people too." He laughed, catching my eye in the mirror. "Come on out, Lynley. Time to meet the troops."

I slipped out of the truck and went around to the back to join the group. Introductions were made, but don't ask me to remember the names—my brain was too busy questioning what I could do that these skilled professionals couldn't.

I was nervous, but I didn't have much time to dwell on it—next thing I knew, I was edging down the cement walkway behind Special Agent Lee with the videographer Damon on my tail. *Don't talk loudly, laugh, swear, or make derogatory remarks*, I reminded myself. Not that I would, but the thought that I might blurt something out accidentally made me even more ill at ease.

When we got to the door, Lee rang the bell then knocked loudly. "Northwest Humane Investigators," she announced in her basso voice. Though female, she was a big girl with an imposing manner, and I wondered at the intelligence of sending her into this delicate situation as its first representative.

The door cracked an inch or two. "Whadda you want?" shot a woman who I presumed to be Judy Smith.

Lee poked the warrant through the crack, then began to explain what they were about to do.

"No *flocking* way!" was Smith's unambiguous response.

She attempted to slam the door in Lee's face, but the special agent deftly stopped it with a well-placed boot. In a calm but assertive voice, Lee continued her account.

Judy Smith was having none of it. I could see by the crimson hue creeping into her puffy face that Agent Lee was only making things worse.

Stepping forward, I said softly, "Connie…" I intentionally used the agent's first name… "Why don't you let me talk to Judy for a minute."

Agent Lee gave me an incredulous stare.

"That's why Denny brought me, remember?"

"Uh, okay, Lynley, but I'll be right here."

That settled, I turned to the woman, Judy. From what I could see of her, she seemed like an unobtrusive matron in a brown tunic over baggy pink leggings. From around her neck hung a small pendant, a black background with streaks of white in a pleasing geometric design.

I felt a shiver of excitement. "That's a Volana Kote, isn't it?" I said with a smile.

Letting the door fall open a bit wider, she put her hand to the pendant. "Why yes. My Tigger. He passed some time ago, but I wear it always. You know of Moon Kitten?"

"Yes, of course. I have a few of her tribute pendants myself." The craftsperson who made beautiful jewelry utilizing naturally fallen whiskers was renowned among cat people.

"I'm Lynley Cannon," I said, building on the shared familiarity of the pendant maker. "I wonder if we could talk. Do you mind if we go inside?"

Judy squinted at me with red rimmed eyes, then her gaze slipped to the cop and the video camera. "What about them?"

"Just me." I fired a pleading look at the agent. "I'll be fine."

Lee considered for a moment, then nodded. "We'll be here. Don't be long."

Judy stood aside, and I stepped into the house. As the door closed behind me, I felt a momentary twinge of anxiety, but then I saw the cats and remembered why I was there.

As Denny had warned me, the place was a mess and the stench of cat urine overpowering. Judy offered me a seat, but I chose to remain standing—I loved cats but that didn't mean I wanted to sit on her pee-stained sofa.

"Well, Lynley Cannon, are you here to take away my cats? Because if you are, you might as well get out right now. My cats are my life. I'm not giving them up to some shelter who's going to turn around and euthanize them. They may not have the cushiest of lives here…" She stared miserably at the meowing hoard. "It has become kinda crowded, what with people dropping off new ones all the time and Miss Marbles having kittens—but they're better off here than dead!" she declared emphatically.

"No one's going to harm your cats," I assured her. "In

fact, just the opposite. Those folks out there only want what's best for them." I peered around, noting more signs of cat overpopulation, to say nothing of the cats themselves—a scraggy, scruffy lot. Some had noticeable wounds, and the sneezing and snuffling denoted an upper respiratory infection running rampant. "You mentioned yourself that it was getting crowded. Northwest Humane can take some of the cats off your hands and get them adopted into good homes. Then the remaining ones wouldn't be such a burden for you."

Judy eyed me skeptically. "I don't believe you."

I sighed. How could I convince this woman who was clearly unstable when it came to her cats?

"I have nine cats myself," I said out of the blue.

Her small eyes widened. "You do?"

"Yes. Sometimes it's hard, especially providing them with medical care, but I've worked out how to swing it."

"Some of mine could use medical care." She sighed and peered about forlornly. "But I'm on a fixed income. Going to the vet is so costly—there's no way..."

"I get it. It's expensive. But it's necessary." I felt a prick on my ankle and looked down at the tiny black spot—a flea. Brushing it off with my other foot, I asked, "You want to keep them healthy, don't you?"

She plopped down onto the soiled sofa and grabbed a small calico to her chest.

"You're not having them," she grumbled into the brightly colored fur.

"What if we could come up with a compromise? Maybe take the cats to NWHS for medical care, then once your house is cleaned up and you've had some time to think, see about returning a smaller, more manageable number and putting others up for adoption."

"You'd make them well again?"

I nodded. "The vets can take care of their URI, treat any wounds and abscesses, and give them a thorough checkup." I flicked another flea off my foot and added before I could stop myself, "And get rid of these damnable fleas!"

"They wouldn't kill any of them?"

"No, of course not."

"And they'd give them back to me once they were fixed?"

"That would depend on you, but yes, I think that could happen. Not all, but maybe two or three. You'd have to work that out with the arbitrator."

Her hand moved to a black cat perched listlessly on the arm of the sofa. He sneezed, showering her with mucus which she wiped off on her leggings.

"I never meant to have so many. People just keep giving them to me. The crazy cat lady is what they call me." She laughed. "I guess that's what I am."

She stared around once more, then her gaze settled on me. "Okay, I'll talk to that guy, Agent Paris. I'm not making any promises, but maybe we can work something out after all."

I left the house, glad to be out of the stench. Special Agent Lee escorted me back to the group where I relayed the conversation to Denny.

"I hope I did the right thing," I finished up. "She just wants what's best for the cats."

"If that's true," said Denny, "then it's something we can work with. We don't want to cause her any more grief than we have to, but the cats' safety comes first."

I sat in the truck while Denny went to parley further with Judy Smith. I felt exhausted, as if I'd run a marathon.

My ankle burned where the flea had connected, and just the idea of those nasty bugs made me itch in other places as well.

I couldn't stop thinking about Judy—and about Darla. *Crazy Cat Lady. Too many cats.* "*People just keep giving them to me,*" Judy had said. Darla related something similar when she arrived home with Newberry. I knew what that was about—when one gets a reputation for caring for cats, the appeals start coming in from every corner. *My friend is moving and can't take her cats... I found this sweet stray but can't adopt him myself... My cat had kittens—will you take one... pleeease?* I got those entreaties all the time, but by steering them to other agencies, I'd figured out how to say no. Obviously both Judy and Darla had yet to learn that lesson.

Hopefully Judy would listen to reason and get her life back in order. Darla was another matter. She was doing well at the moment, but what would happen if she continued to take more cats every time someone had a need? Would she realize her limitations, or would she end up in a pee-stained, flea-bitten mess like poor Judy Smith?

Chapter 12

Cats have an instinctive routine: play (hunt-catch-kill), eat, groom, and sleep. Keep your cat happy by indulging these four basic needs.

"Up a little bit—no, not that way, the other up!"

I stopped the sigh of exasperation that welled in my throat and did as my mother asked. Only Carol Mackay would invent a direction called the *other* up! Leaning precariously to the left on the little stepladder, I shifted the Terrace Traders sign an inch higher, then forced a smile.

"How's that?"

Carol stared thoughtfully, arms crossed over her calico smock, and *hmmmed*.

"Is that a good *hmmm* or a bad *hmmm*? Really, Mum, I can't hold this position much longer."

"Oh, Lynley, get on down from there. I'll do it myself."

"No, you won't," I shot back. "There's no way I'm letting you climb a ladder, even a short one."

For a moment, we glared at each other, then she turned away. "I suppose it will have to do. It's only a slight bit crooked."

Taking her at her word, I pinned the placard to the backboard and got down before she could change her mind.

"No one will notice," I cajoled. "They'll be too busy perusing all the lovely things you and the other ladies from the Terrace have up for sale."

"You're probably right," Carol conceded. "We do have some nice things, don't we? But we're not all ladies, dear. Bob crochets the scarves, and Mr. Tibbets does those sweet dioramas of tiny gothic libraries. Colin and his husband Roland made all the wooden children's toys…"

"You're right, Mum. Sorry."

Carol scanned the pile of totes stacked in a corner of the booth. "Do you think we'll have enough?"

"More to the point is, will we get it all set out by closing tonight?" I panned the big room, now abustle with other makers, crafters, and vendors doing the same thing we were—setting up their booths for tomorrow's opening of the Hawthorne All-Hallows Holiday Festival.

It had been two days since my adventure with Special Agent Paris and the hoarder Judy Smith. I was curious about the outcome but knew those things took time. Denny would fill me in when he had something to relate. Meanwhile the fête was upon us—Carol with her crafts booth, and Seleia rehearsing for their play—so I had other things on my mind.

I caught Carol watching a hand truck stacked high with plastic bins wobble toward us on a landing vector. All I could see of the pusher was a hand braced on the top bin in a hopeless attempt to keep the whole thing from toppling. The truck pulled up at the booth with a clunk, and out from behind the haphazard tower stepped Carol's roommate Candy.

Candy Hemmingway had lived with my mother for longer than I could remember, to the point where they tended to emulate one another in little gestures and acts. A nod of the head, an often-used phrase, Candy was a plumpish mirror of Carol.

"Whew," she heaved, sinking into the folding chair.

"That was no fun. I had to park all the way around the block, and it's raining again. Really hard! I probably wouldn't have made it if Fredric hadn't helped me into the building."

I gave a look around for the young man.

"Oh, he had to go to the auditorium," said Candy. "Rehearsals for the play. But he said he'd stop by later to see if we needed help with anything, such as climbing ladders and hanging things."

Carol glanced at the sign I'd just risked my life to affix. "We could use…" she began, but I shot her a black look. "No, I suppose we're good on that, but it was nice for him to offer.

Candy flipped open the lid of the nearest tote and peered inside. "Shall we start putting things out?"

"Yes, definitely," Carol affirmed, puckering her brow. "We have a lot of work ahead of us. Lynley, you can begin by…"

"Look!" I interrupted. "It's Harlene! She must have got a space after all. Think I'll go say hello. You ladies can handle the rest of the setup by yourselves, right?"

I didn't wait for an answer but took off across the room to the Pet Pantry booth. There was no way I wanted to get in the middle of Carol and Candy bickering about how to lay out the space and where to place their items. Not that I didn't appreciate what the pair was doing—donating part of their proceeds to Friends of Felines—but I knew from experience that I would be more hindrance than help when it came to arranging the beaded jewelry, purses made of gum wrappers, embroidered mottos, costumes for pets, and other whimsies that came from the hobbies of the retired.

I was on my way to Harlene's booth when I heard my

name and turned.

"Seleia!" I greeted my granddaughter with a little hug. "I thought you were in rehearsals."

"We are, but it's break, and I wanted to come see what you were doing down here..." Her gaze edged to the side, to a flamboyant man standing a little behind her. "...and to introduce you to Kiefer—Kiefer Clark, the director of *Dream*."

Clark stepped forward with the charm of a seasoned pro. A little taller than Seleia, he was a compact man with all the right dimensions. Dark, gray-flecked hair fell around his face in an attractively unkempt manner that matched a well-groomed five o'clock shadow. His sensuous lips looked like they smiled easily, and his smokey eyes sported full lashes that I'd swear were artificially lengthened. A lovingly well-worn cashmere sports coat over a red checked Pendleton shirt topped off by a raw silk scarf around his neck gave him the air of a man who dresses well but in his own style.

Extending a hand, he uttered a predictable, "Seleia has told me so much about you."

I took the hand—warm, pleasant, friendly. "Pleased to meet you too. How is the play coming?"

His eyes lit. "Wonderfully! I mean, as well as can be expected—wouldn't want to jinx it by bragging. Still some work to be done, of course. And your granddaughter here is a gem. Such raw talent!"

Seleia nearly trembled with pride as she slipped just a scooch closer to the dynamic man, furthering my concern that her feelings for the director were growing beyond a generic respect. To his credit, he didn't seem to notice, or if he did, he was doing a good job of hiding it.

"Ah, there's Charles!" he exclaimed. "I must go have a

chat. It was nice meeting you, Ms. Cannon. I do hope to see you at the performance."

"I wouldn't miss it."

"Catch you after rehearsal, Grandmother, if you're still here."

I glanced at the Terrace Trader's booth where Carol and Candy were arguing about the placement of a papier mâché cat. "I'm not sure about me, but Granna and Candy will be here until the wee hours. Drop by and give them some encouragement if you have time."

"I'll try. Ciao, Lynley."

Seleia took off behind her mentor, trailing along like a cat after a string. I wondered if I should be worried, but Kiefer Clark seemed to have his wits about him, and aside from praising her talent, he hadn't reciprocated her flirtation in the least. Besides, I had a feeling Seleia wasn't his type. She would be disappointed, but I doubted it would end in heartbreak.

I continued to Harlene's booth where the round woman was struggling with a promotional banner that was meant to drape between the two outer poles of a canopy.

"Grab that other end, will you Lynley?" she said the moment she saw me.

I did as bid, and together we easily hung the colorful sign. Standing back, we admired our handiwork, then greeted each other in a more proper fashion.

"I see you got a spot," I commented.

"Last minute, but I wangled it somehow. If you hadn't reminded me, I probably would have forgotten all about it."

Harlene shuffled through a box full of Christmas decorations, finally drawing out a round Tupperware container. Snapping the lid, I smelled the most delicious combination of cinnamon and spice.

"You're not going to tell me those are for cats."

She held the container out to me. "Have one. My uncle's secret recipe but vegan. He called them elves' hats, but they're really just spice cookies."

I took one of the delicacies and popped it in my mouth. The tiny cookie melted into a pleasure of flavors. "Mmmm," I murmured. "If I were a baker, I'd have to pester you for the recipe."

"You can have it if you want. It was his secret, not mine."

"Thanks, but it would be wasted on me. Baking isn't my talent, I'm afraid."

Harlene took another cookie, then set the tub on the table. "Help yourself," she remarked. "I made a quadruple recipe to get me through the holiday." Turning to her pile of boxes, she placed her hands on her ample hips. "Now, where to begin?"

"I see you plan to keep up the Christmas theme."

"Absolutely. So far I'm the only one in the place with Christmassy decor."

"I believe it. There's a reason for that, you know—it isn't Christmas yet!"

"I thought I explained it to you, dear."

"You did, but it's still hard to wrap my head around. Let's just make it through Halloween first, okay?"

She shrugged, sending the sleeve of her red and green apron off her shoulder. She pulled it back up. "You'll see. I bet I sell more than anyone else in this room."

"I hope you do—except for my mother's booth. She and her group of senior crafters are first-timers, and I'd love to see them make a killing."

Harlene looked pensive.

"What?" I asked.

"Such a funny idiom—to make a killing. Downright gruesome when you think about it."

I did think about it and agreed she was right. "I don't know what made me say that—I've probably been watching too much classic TV. Now I'd better get back to Carol before she and her roommate get into a knock-down drag-out about where to hang the macramé."

I was about to go when I saw a familiar figure over the top of Harlene's shoulder. How could anyone miss the lithe young woman in the rainbow caftan and orange-red hair?

"What is it, Lynley? You look like you've seen a ghost."

"No, nothing like that. It's my new employer, Darla. Did I tell you I'm cat sitting now? She's my first client." Harlene followed my gaze and her eyes widened. "She's not as odd as she looks," I said, then paused in thought. "At least I don't think she is."

Harlene turned her stare on me, her sky-blue eyes wide as a surprised cat. "You're working for *her*?"

I caught the emphasis on the pronoun but didn't understand it. "Yes. I've done it a couple of times now. She just lives around the block..."

Harlene grabbed my arm and led me to the corner of the booth, out of Darla's sightline though the woman was across the hall and had yet to notice me.

"Have you met her partner?" Harlene whispered.

"Partner? No. I didn't know she had one. She never said anything to me about it."

"Partner, boyfriend, cohort—whatever you want to call him, he's creepy. She shops at the store—comes in every week or so."

"I'm not surprised. She has as many cats as I do."

"Only once did she bring the man, but once was enough."

I instantly thought of the muffled male voice on the answering machine. "Why? What happened?"

She drew me in a little farther. "Well, you know how she usually dresses in those brilliant, outlandish colors? That time she was all in black, like a nun without the white parts. Him too—black coat, trousers, hat."

"Lots of people dress in black. This is Portland, after all."

"That's not the strange part. It was the conversation I overheard. He was talking to her about giving shots to a cat, and it wasn't the veterinarian-prescribed kind!"

"What do you mean? Like cannabis or CBD?"

Harlene shrugged. "I don't know. I just heard him say the drugs were illegal. He sort of snickered, then he said it didn't matter that they were painful—he'd inject the cat whether she liked it or not."

"But that's terrible! He must have been joking. All Darla's cats seem happy and healthy, certainly not high." Then I hesitated. Was that the reason her clowder slept so much? Had she been drugging them into a stupor? But no—I'd seen enough cats come back from the vet after various procedures to know what the effects of anesthesia looked like. "At least they seemed fine when I was there."

"I got the feeling he was talking about one cat in particular. Maybe it was his cat, not hers. Either way, giving animals medicines not approved for them by their doctor is wrong, just wrong!"

"I agree, but maybe you misunderstood what he was saying."

"Maybe, but I still don't like him. And I don't trust her. You be careful if you keep working for her."

With that, Harlene gave a little shimmy as if to shake off the bad vibes and grabbed a table covering from the topmost box. "Now help me get this on straight, will you Lynley?" she asked, back to her old jovial self.

Together we got the huge holly-print cloth placed just right on the long table. I was about to bid Harlene farewell for a second time when there came the earsplitting screech of car tires from outside the building. The squeal was instantly followed by the nauseating crunch of vehicles slamming into each other. There was another crash and yet another. A horn blared and stuck. Then came the screams.

By this time, everyone in the hall was staring at the far wall, as if by sheer willpower, they could see what disaster had transpired on the other side. Some folks were already running for the door, making their way out to gawk or help or just bear witness. As they passed me, their faces blank with anticipatory fear, I found myself joining them. Suddenly there was nothing so important as finding out what had made those horrific sounds.

As we left the exhibit hall, the shouts grew louder, and the whine of the stuck horn became unbearable. In the busy cross street was a mangle of cars, one on its side and another with a front end so crumpled as to be caved in entirely. The door of a beat-up old Chevy truck clashed open, falling off its hinges into the street. The driver stumbled out, a dazed figure wrapped in what looked like a strip of blue tarp material.

The hapless man staggered through the crashed cars as if lost. His drawn face was as pale and gray as the October sky. His bare shoulders and calves were thin and skeletal. With glazed eyes, he stared unseeingly at the ground.

After only a few steps, he toppled, sinking to one knee, then both. Pitching forward with a breathless groan, he did a faceplant into a puddle on the pavement where he lay as if dead.

Onlookers were already rushing to his assistance, shouting conflicting orders: "Get him up!" "No, don't move him!" "Wait for the ambulance." "My God! This man looks like he's been through hell!"

Someone got the horn unstuck, and there was a brief moment of silence before a new cacophony of horn blasts started up, unwitting drivers angry at the jam that had brought the busy intersection to a standstill. I heard the scream of sirens as both the police and the medical team arrived, each on opposite sides of the collision. While the medics made their way to assist the injured, the police got busy corralling the onlookers, of which I was one.

It was time to go back into the building and let the authorities do their grisly job. Walking slowly, I wondered if anyone was badly hurt… if anyone had died. What could have caused such a horrendous accident on an inner city thoroughfare? Was it the driving rain or something more sinister?

I paused just inside the big double doors. I felt lightheaded, as if I'd been part of the turmoil myself. Then I felt a touch on my arm.

"Lynley dear, are you alright?"

Blinking away tears I hadn't known were there, I saw my mother peering at me with concern.

"I'm fine, Mum. I'm not sure about those other people…" I waved a limp hand toward the pileup. "Did you see?"

"No, but Candy did. She was outside when it happened. She told me he just drove through the red light, and everybody collided with each other trying not to hit him."

"He? Who?"

"Candy recognized him right off, though she said he's lost a lot of weight and looks absolutely frightful. It's Geraldine's nephew Gerald." Carol took a deep breath. "Gerald Sullivan, one of the Lost Boys."

"Lost boys?" I wasn't tracking. What did Peter Pan have to do with a man in a blue tarp who'd caused a ten-car crash?

"That's what they're calling them in the news media now."

"Them, who?" I was becoming frustrated with my mother's tendency to be obscure.

Carol gave me an exasperated look. "Why, the young men who've gone missing along the I-5 corridor, of course."

Chapter 13

Petting a cat can be calming, even in the direst of situations.

Within the exhibition hall, the vendors were solemn and silent as they went about the business of finishing their setup. The tragedy we'd witnessed cast a shroud of gloom over the place, and everyone merely wanted to get out of there, home to their families and loved ones, which in my case meant my cats.

I helped Carol and Candy place the rest of their wares, a hurried affair, leaving any finishing touches for the morning before the grand opening at noon. At that point, even Carol didn't care if it wasn't perfect. She hastily tossed a cover over the table, and we headed for the door.

Outside we were met with full dark, the premature night of a stormy late October. The police were still clearing the accident site that had blocked the busy intersection. A tow truck hefted the broken Chevy onto its long bed, and another was just leaving. One lane had been cleared, so traffic was getting through but at a snail's pace, an unwelcome surprise for the rush hour travelers.

People at the bus stop across the street fixed their eyes on the activity, while others bustled in and out of the Fred Meyer store with furtive glances at the scene. I turned away, pulling up my collar against the wind and rain as well as the ominous pall that hovered over the scene of devastation.

"Where are you parked?" Carol asked me.

"Around the block by the bank. How about you?"

"Us too," said Candy. "We can walk together."

In silence, the three of us set out for our cars without looking back.

Impulsively Carol grabbed my arm. "How about coming over to ours for a visit, dear? Candy's made some yummy lemon scones. We could have tea."

At first, I was surprised by my mother's outburst, but when I looked in her eyes and saw the sorrow there, I understood. What we'd witnessed—me, the horrendous accident and the collapse of the emaciated man in the scrap of blue tarp, and she, the chaotic aftermath—was burned into our minds just as a bright light imprints its image on the retina. The awful scenes would fade in time, but making new, loving memories was a way to diminish that horror today.

* * *

Half an hour later Carol, Candy, and I were sitting in their warm condo sipping tea and nibbling on Candy's delicious scones. Carol's Persian cat Priss had settled in the old woman's lap the moment she sat down, adding fluffy comfort to the cozy scene. The view from their windows overlooked the city where the lights from cars and buildings sparkled in the rain. There, in that place of peace high above the streets, we could pretend everything was fine, that people weren't hurting, that strange things didn't happen. At least we could try.

But soon we ran out of small talk. After a third awkward silence, Carol grabbed the remote from the coffee table and clicked on the television set. It immediately went to the local news, as she knew it would. Neither Candy nor I objected to this blatant disruption of our impromptu tea party. We all wanted the same thing—answers.

Sure enough, the anchorwoman was standing in the very place we had vacated only an hour before. Behind her, we could see the tangled mess of the pileup. Then a photo box flashed up in the corner of the screen, a nice-looking young man smiling for the camera. The picture was familiar to anyone who lived in the Pacific Northwest. They had been seeing it on the news, on the web, and even on telephone poles for some time—Gerald Sullivan, the first man to go missing of the group that was now being called the I-5 Lost Boys.

A new photo came on the screen, blurry and out of focus. Could it possibly be the same man?

"Turn it up!" Candy charged, and Carol complied.

"...in the first news of the missing men, Gerald Sullivan was recovered today in Southeast Portland. Unfortunately, Mr. Sullivan fell unconscious before he could give any information about what had happened to him. He was rushed to OHSU where he remains in critical condition."

"So it was Gerald," Candy moaned. "Even though I was certain, I prayed it wasn't true. Where has he been for the past months?"

"Shhh!" Carol hissed. "Maybe they'll tell us if you'd be quiet for a moment."

Candy put a hand over her mouth, and we all turned back to the television set.

"Sullivan was first reported missing two months ago. Since then, three other men, Guy Ward, Barry Campbell, and Jon Wyatt Flatt have also disappeared. All four young men are of similar demographics and reside within the Portland-Seattle corridor, which has earned them the nickname of the I-5 Lost Boys. But these are not boys—they are men between the ages of twenty and twenty-eight. They are all well-respected, with jobs, families, and friends who noticed their absence immediately. The most recent departure was last Sunday. There are still no leads as to who might be doing this, or why. Any information about these horrendous crimes can be reported on the following tipline or given to Police Chief Bryant at the number on your screen."

The news anchor fell silent, putting a hand to her ear bud as she listened intently. When she again faced the camera, her face was drawn and somber.

"We have just learned that Gerald Sullivan died soon after arriving at the hospital. He was badly malnourished and suffering from hypothermia. Marks on his ankles indicate that he was bound and had been so for a very long time."

"I can't watch any more." I stood and turned away.

The sound clicked off, leaving an echoing silence. I stared out the window at the scene below, a string of lights crossing the Hawthorne Bridge like rows of red and white fireflies. Something about their calm, flowing passage felt soothing.

"I'd better go," I said, returning to the couch where I had stashed my purse. "I still don't know when I'm supposed to be cat sitting for Darla. She said it would be later this week but didn't give a day."

"That's not very considerate of her," Carol decreed. "You do have a life of your own."

"I know," I sighed. "And I'm not planning to jump at her command, but... well, it is just around the block. If she needs me..."

Carol pulled herself to her feet, displacing Priss who

merely shifted her affections to Candy. As she walked me to the door, she said, "Don't be a washrag, dear."

"I think you mean dishcloth, but no, I won't do anything I don't want to do."

"That's my girl." Carol patted me on the back as if I were a sports figure and she was my coach. "And try not to let what we saw today get you down. Bad things happen."

"I know. It's just that I'm not usually there to see them up close and personal. The thought of the missing men is just plain disturbing."

Carol nodded. "You're right about that. What has our peaceful little Portland come to?"

"'Bye, Candy," I called over Carol's shoulder. "Thanks for the tea and pastries."

"You're welcome, dear," came the prescribed response. "It was lovely to see you." We were back to the veneer of politeness that served to buffer the heartbreaks of the world.

"You'll join us tomorrow at the hall?" Carol instructed more than asked.

"I'll be there. Love you. Mum..." I added, giving her a little hug. "You can count on me."

I made a quick retreat before she could grab me with another demand, critical remark, or piece of advice. Love with my mother could be a double-edged sword.

The rain was coming down harder than ever, and throughout the short drive from the Terrace to my house, I was constantly adjusting my glasses trying to make out the cars on the road. The good part was that the white-knuckled trip had taken my undivided concentration, which in turn kept me from thinking about the accident and the poor dead man in the blue tarp scrap, but once I got home, the images resurged.

Who was this cruel kidnapper terrorizing our area? I couldn't help but wonder. But then another thought eclipsed the first: *A kidnapper no longer, whoever was doing this had just promoted themselves to the ranks of murderer as well.*

Chapter 14

Cats have different dietary requirements depending on age, weight, and medical conditions. To learn exactly what your cat needs, check with your vet.

The call came just as I finished feeding the cats. Little gave a sideways glance when the phone rang, but no one else bothered to look up from their fare.

"Sorry for the short notice," Darla said breathlessly. "I did mention I might need you. Are you up for a kitty sit?"

Holding the phone, I stepped in front of Big Red who was heading over to see if Emilio's cuisine might be superior to his own.

"No, sweetie," I told the big tabby. "It's all the same food."

"Pardon?"

"Sorry, I was talking to my cat. When would you need me?"

"Well, now? I'm actually in Seattle. I meant to call earlier, but things just got away from me."

I turned and leaned against the counter, keeping an eye on Red. "So you just left your cats without making arrangements?" I caught a snarky tinge to my voice and took a breath.

"They'll be fine if you can't come," she said petulantly. "But I know they would enjoy the company."

"Sure," I sighed. "I've got nothing else to do tonight."

There was a pause. "Are you okay, Lynley? You sound

fraught."

Fraught? It was an old-fashioned term, but it did rather hit the nail on the head.

"I guess I am. There was a big accident today down by the Masonic Hall. I didn't witness it, but I saw the results. It was pretty gruesome."

"That's terrible. Was everyone alright?"

"Not really..." I didn't finish. I didn't want to talk about the dead man. I didn't want to think about him. Most of all, I didn't want to imagine what those other Lost Boys might be going through at that very moment.

"When will you be back?" I blurted, a blatant evasion.

"Tomorrow night, if all goes well."

I didn't ask what she meant—I didn't care. At that moment, all I could think about was going to do my job, pet some cats, come home, and go to bed, hopefully to feel better in the morning.

"Okay, I'll go look in on them after I have some dinner."

"Thank you so much, You're a godsend..."

"It's okay this time, but Darla," I put in, "I would appreciate more notice in the future. For your sake," I added. "I'm not always free."

That was a stretch of the truth. My schedule was my own to arrange any way I wanted, but she didn't have to know that. As my mother had told me in such colorful language, I shouldn't be a washrag, a dishcloth, or a doormat—not for anyone.

Most of the cats had finished eating and were on to their grooming stage. Violet still hunkered by her bowl, the overweight cat hoping it would magically grow more food. Tinkerbelle, who ate like a princess, nibbled at the last of her morsels. Big Red approached her hopefully, and she gave him a throaty growl. Tink may have been tiny, but she was fierce.

I took a vegan taco bowl out of the freezer and popped it into the microwave. While it was heating, I gathered the things I needed for the cat sitting visit—nothing much since I didn't intend to stay long. Still, the thought of sitting with Oscar and Gloria made me smile. I hadn't smiled since the accident, and it felt good. I decided to run with it.

Twenty minutes later, I tossed the paper bowl into the compost bin and packed my thermos of after-dinner tea in my tote. That, and my current mystery book, was all I needed.

"Be home soon," I told my cats as I slipped out the back door.

I headed for Darla's, pausing only once at a neighboring property where a wild, overgrown garden nearly obscured the house within. The tenant kept chickens, big healthy birds she treated as pets. I loved watching them hunt and peck through the tangles of grapevines and flowering currant, but it was late, and the birds had gone to bed. For a moment, I enjoyed picturing them in their little a-frame coop, all cozied up for the night.

The rain had quit for the time being, leaving only shimmering droplets to adorn every branch and tree. As I turned away, my shoulder hit an errant vine, releasing a shower of raindrops on my head. One slipped down my back, sending shivers up my spine. The tiny shock to my system brought me back to reality, and I continued my short trek, head down and glum.

As the Cat House came into view, I saw that Darla had added a trio of very large and uniquely carved Halloween pumpkins to her front yard decorations. They were cat faces, round and sweet and not a bit scary. Climbing the porch, I noted they were lit with battery candles that glimmered and glowed like the real thing, only safer.

All the interior lights were off, including the fairy lights. Letting myself in with the key, I felt for the wall switch. When I flicked it on, the place lit up like a holiday, revealing myriad pairs of blinking eyes, all pointed at me.

"Hello, Kitties," I greeted. Somebody meowed back, but the rest were silent.

Shedding my coat, I dropped my tote on the couch, then made a tour of the room, trying to remember everybody's names. I picked out Oscar on the window ledge and Gloria in her table bed. Timmy and Tommy were curled together in a wide wicker basket. *Hans, Freyja, Webster, Billy, Léonard,* I recited as I sought them out cat by cat. *But where is the new one—Newberry?* I wondered. Did Darla still have her separated in her bedroom? Maybe the young woman was learning about cats after all.

Once I'd checked to make sure the food dispenser was working properly and the water fountain was clean, I went to find Newberry. The bedroom door was open, but a screen door had been installed so the cat could look out without having unwanted feline intrusions on her personal space.

Another point for Darla, I thought to myself. If nothing else, she was a fast learner.

Newberry sprawled on the bed like a queen. This was the first time I'd seen the whole of her, and she was indeed beautiful—mottled dove gray and white with long, silky fur so dense it grew in tufts between her pretty toes. She slow-blinked those great golden eyes, and I blinked back.

Taking it as an invitation, I slipped in the gate and

gave a brief look around the room, noting it was now outfitted with a smaller version of the automatic feeder and a tiny fountain shaped like a flower. The litter box was the old fashioned kind and rather on the full side, so after a quick pet fest with the lady of the house, I cleaned it, disposed of the bag in the bathroom receptacle, and washed my hands.

"Now, Newberry," I said, sitting softly on the bed. "How are you enjoying your new home?"

Newberry gave another lingering blink, then stood, stretched, and walked into my lap where she curled up once more.

"I guess you got over that shyness thing, didn't you?"

I petted down her back—she was a bit on the thin side but not unhealthily so—and was answered with the softest of purrs. I had to wonder about the shelter that had deemed this cat unadoptable. Unless there was something I was missing, a fatal disease or an unresolvable behavior issue, she seemed perfectly fine to me.

Then I wondered about Darla's friend, the person who had asked Darla to take Newberry in the first place. Darla hadn't mentioned the name of the shelter, but I knew that at FOF, such a thing would not have been possible. Cats were either adopted through their system, officially transferred to another shelter, or in the case of one so ill as to be beyond recovery, the vets took a vote on humane euthanasia to end their suffering. No one could just decide to give a cat away on a whim.

"You're special, aren't you?" I crooned.

Newberry looked up at me as if she understood, which she probably did.

Suddenly I felt her body tense. Her eyes went wide as she stared at the far wall. Then I heard it too, a soft moaning, coming from nearby.

I sat rigid, listening, but now there was only silence and the far-away rhythmic crunching of someone eating at the feeder in the living room. I'd almost convinced myself I'd been hearing things when it came again, a little louder this time. It sounded like someone in pain.

Newberry catapulted from my lap, crouched low on the floor, then slunk like a lioness stalking prey toward the wall shared with the demon room. Once there, she froze, staring at the baseboard with her ears pricked forward. I followed and pressed my ear against the plaster. I heard... nothing.

"I'm going to check this out," I said in a whisper though I wasn't sure why. "Back in a minute. You stay here." This got a dubious look from Newberry and an admonishment from myself. Where else was she going to go?

It was nerves. The moan I was almost certain I'd heard was so very like the groan of Gerald Sullivan when he collapsed in the street. I would never forget that sound, possibly one of the last utterances he made before he died. What did Darla have locked away in that room that could make such a noise?

Then a thought hit me square between the eyes. It was ludicrous, impossible, but despite its outlandishness, it lodged itself in my paranoid brain and stuck. No way could cat lady Darla be the I-5 Abductor... could she?

I slipped out of Newberry's bedroom, softly closing the gate behind me. Creeping up to the blue door, I paused. Once again, I read the little hand-penned sign, "No go in." The wording seemed strange. The common, "Do not enter," or even the slightly rude, "Keep Out!" would have been more typical. And the demon in the painting was even weirder. Small, twisted body, big head, wayward hair, and a single black eye that seemed to stare straight at the viewer. I moved from side to side—the painted gaze followed. I knew it was a trick of the artist capturing the eye in such a way that it gave the impression of contact, but it was disconcerting nonetheless.

I stepped nearer and placed my ear on the cool wood panel. At first, I heard nothing but the rush of my blood echoing through my head. Then softly, slowly, a sound began to mount—a moan so ghostly as to make me feel like running away screaming and never turning back.

But I was a big girl, and one with the curiosity of a cat, so all I did was step away to regroup. As I lingered in the shadow at the end of Darla's hallway, I thought it out, piece by piece.

There is something in that room, I calculated. *Something that moans. But is it a moan, as from a living being? It might not be a moan at all. It could be the wind. At my house, the wind in the overhead wires keens like a banshee. But it's not windy outside. Hmmm.*

With sudden conviction, I made up my mind. Reaching quickly before I could think better of it, I grabbed the doorknob. Twisting it, I felt the latch give way. It moved the slightest bit, but no farther. The door was locked.

A locked door wasn't about to appease my curiosity, though. I wouldn't be happy until I knew what was making that noise. And more to the point, I wouldn't feel safe until I confirmed it wasn't human. The wild notion that Darla could be the I-5 Kidnapper was beyond ridiculous, but I had to see for myself, if for no other reason than to banish the thought from my mind.

Retreating down the hall, I bee-lined through the living

room to the front door. Making sure I had the keys and my phone, I stepped outside. It was cold, and I considered going back for my coat—or just going back and staying put with the cats—but it was too late. I was on a mission.

I followed the stepping stone walk through the gnome garden, around the catio to the corner of the house. A brick path paralleled the outer wall, and I took it. As I passed the living room window, I glanced inside to see the cats all comfy in their beds. A few were watching me, and again I thought about turning around, but my feet kept walking.

I found the high window that I judged to be the one in the secret room, but even standing on my tiptoes, I was too short to see in. With the help of the windowsill, I tried hefting myself up, but all that did was to tax my deconditioned arm muscles—my *hefting* ship had sailed a decade ago. Frustrated, I jumped as high as I could, then repeated the hopping motion, but to no avail. When I slipped and nearly fell on my backside in the wet leaves, I decided I needed a different, and safer, approach.

I'd noticed a step ladder on Darla's porch and headed back to retrieve it. Skirting the gnomes, I glanced in at the cats who, no longer interested in my antics, were sleeping one and all. It had begun to drizzle, the kind of rain that led up to a storm, so I needed to hustle. By the time I got the little wooden ladder situated beneath the window, I was out of breath.

I gave myself a moment to recover, but I didn't want to waste time in case a helpful neighbor glanced out their window and mistook me for a thief. Carefully bracing the ladder against the wall, I climbed just high enough to peer inside.

The room, a laundry room, was dark save for a single dim sconce over a sink. At first, I could see nothing but the usual furnishings—washer, dryer, sorting table. A long counter with shelves ran up one side of the room, but instead of soaps and bleach, the shelves held a row of flattened towels. On the wall hung a flatscreen TV. It was playing, though from my vantage point I couldn't see what show.

That must have been what I'd heard—something on the television. I was about to get back down when I caught the flicker of movement. Like a wraith, it drifted ghostlike between the wall and the cabinet where it disappeared, then reappeared on the counter by the sink. It stood for a moment, then launched itself straight at me. I flinched away despite the glass between us. When I turned back, the wraith had vanished .

Again, I heard the moan, long and drawn out. There was something familiar about that sound, and I was just putting it together when a face popped into the window directly in front of me, the face of a Siamese cat.

Of course! It all made sense now! Siamese were known for their odd, human-like vocalizations. My own Siamese kitten Mab had a whole range of noises not uttered by any other breed.

The cat was silhouetted against the backlight so I couldn't pick out details, but it seemed like there was something wrong with her color. She was light, a seal or fawn point, but the face itself showed up as yellow. I blinked and looked again, trying to make it into a more normal color but couldn't.

Judging from the thin features and ultra-wide eyes, the little Siamese couldn't have been over a year old. She peered at me for a moment, then her mouth opened in a meow. I touched the glass, and the cat put her nose against it just there.

"What are you in for, sweetheart?" I said, though I knew she couldn't hear me. "Why are you all on your own?"

She made the meow face again, then moved out of sight, materializing once again on the counter where she curled up in the sink, looking yellower than ever against the white of the porcelain. Her face was still turned toward me, and her eyes never left mine.

I watched for a little longer as the eyes closed and she went to sleep, or maybe it was that half-sleep cats assume when they know they are trapped. This one was certainly trapped.

I got down, returned the ladder to its place on the porch, then went back into the house. For a while, I listened for the little Siamese's cry, but the room at the end of the hall was silent. As I spent time with the other cats, giving them attention and love, I found myself pondering my discovery. Why was that one poor cat kept in a locked room? And why the cryptic sign that made her out to be a demon?

Chapter 15

People who love cats often collect cat-related items such as wall art, sculpture, tapestries, jewelry, and coffee mugs. The round, flowing shape of a cat is aesthetically pleasing to the eye.

It was Friday, the first day of the Hawthorne All-Hallows Holiday Festival, and so far, everything was running smoothly. There had been no last minute snafus, no unexpected disasters. Carol and I sat at the back of the Terrace Traders booth sipping tea from thermos cups and watching the very competent Lana Dolittle, a ruddy sixty-something who also lived at The Terrace, hawk their wares to enthusiastic buyers. The sales were going gangbusters, as my mother had mentioned more than once that morning.

There had been a line at the door when we'd arrived to put on the final touches. The weather probably had something to do with it. Yesterday's blusters had abated, and now the sun was out, cold and clear as an icicle. The exhibit hall did not lack for heat, however. As I sipped my hot beverage, I wished I'd worn a tee shirt instead of the black and orange cat-print sweater.

"How was your evening," Carol ventured, now that we had time to talk.

"It was fine," I responded ambiguously. "Darla called just as I got home from your place and asked me to visit her cats."

Carol turned abruptly. "Really? What did you say?"

"What could I say? She was already out of town. Besides, I figured I could use the distraction."

We were silent for a moment, both thinking of the shocking accident and the even more alarming death of the kidnap victim. The night's sleep had buffered the rawness of the shock, but it wasn't something I would forget quickly, and neither would my mother.

"I did have an interesting encounter while I was there."

"Oh? Not another call from the drug pusher, I hope."

"No, nothing like that. I told you about the closed off room with the sign that said not to enter." Carol nodded. "Well, last night I kept hearing noises…"

Carol looked up in alarm. "What sort of noises?"

"Like a moan or a low cry. At first, I thought it was the wind or my imagination, but Newberry heard it too. She's one of Darla's cats," I explained at my mother's blank stare. "It was coming from that room."

"You didn't go in, did you?"

"No, of course not." Carol knew me too well. I lowered my eyes. "I tried, but it was locked."

"Your curiosity gets you nothing but trouble, dear. You should know that by now."

"That's not true, Mum. Sometimes it gets me answers."

"So did it? Get you answers? Because I'm betting you didn't just walk away."

"I couldn't. Something was alive in there, and they might have been hurt or in pain." I declined to mention how much the moans sounded like Gerald Sullivan's final cry before he fainted. And I absolutely refused to admit, even to myself, that for a moment, I had feared the entity in the room was one of the I-5 victims and that Darla was the kidnapper.

"I went outside and looked through the window," I pressed on. "I had to climb on a step ladder because it was high up. You'll never guess what I saw."

"Another cat," she said flatly.

"Yes, but... how did you know?"

Carol smiled smugly. "Strange noises in a house full of cats? Lucky guess."

"That makes sense, though it never crossed my mind until I saw her little face in the window. Her noises were nothing like your standard meows, but she's a Siamese, and they get up to all sorts of sounds." I sighed. "The question is, why is she locked away with a demon sign painted on her door? And why didn't Darla just tell me about her in the first place?"

Carol uncrossed her legs and leaned close to me. "Because your Darla is odd, Lynley. I do wish you'd think twice about working for her. I don't trust her."

"You've never met her."

"No, but sometimes one can just tell."

We both fell silent, immersed in our own thoughts. I was considering what she'd said, wondering if she might be right in her telepathic mother way. I had no idea what she was thinking—probably that I was half insane.

Lana wound up a sale of a long knitted scarf that would do justice to Doctor Who and was turning to another customer perusing the birdhouses.

"Do you need any help?" Carol called out.

The woman turned and gave a grin. "I'm fine, sweet Caroline," she rhymed back in a baritone singsong. "This is my forte! I haven't had so much fun since I quit the carny!"

"The carny?" I asked Carol. "For real?"

"Oh, yes. Lana was a cigarette girl for Barnum and

Bailey back in the day."

I studied the frumpy woman with new appreciation. It always amazed me to learn the things retired people had done in their salad days. My own counterculture youth had been very different from the life I embraced today.

I was lost in thought, remembering the time a group of us had gone skinny-dipping in a private lake and nearly got caught by the owner, when Seleia dashed in all a-fluster.

She grabbed my arm. "Grandmother, have you seen Fredric?"

"Ouch, sweetheart." I pried her fingers from their death grip. "Why? What's the matter?"

"It's nearly time for dress rehearsal, and Fredric hasn't come in yet. He's playing both Lysander and Puck, and if he doesn't get here soon, it'll throw the whole production off."

"I haven't seen him today. Have you, Carol?" The older woman shook her head. "His car was in front of the duplex this morning when I left though." I thought back. "Last night, too. But there weren't any lights on. I figured he might have been out with you."

Seleia looked away. "No, not with me. Except for rehearsal, we haven't seen much of each other lately." She let the implication hang in the overheated air.

"He wouldn't just run out on the play like that, would he?" Carol posed.

Seleia took a moment to answer. "He might. We had a fight."

"Another one?" I asked softly.

She nodded. "I told him I wanted to see other people. He took it pretty hard."

I nearly pushed her as to which other people might she

be referring to, but I figured I already knew. Besides, that wasn't the issue at hand. The question was, would Seleia's rebuke make a seasoned theater and film person run off and leave the show high and dry? *The show must go on* wasn't just an old-fashioned saying—it was an axiom by which actors lived.

"Darn him!" Seleia was exclaiming. "I can't believe he'd be so childish. I don't know what I ever saw in that man!"

She huffed out of the booth, then turned back. "I'm going up to the auditorium. I guess Fredric's understudy will get his chance after all. And if you see Fredric, tell him he can go to..."

"We'll tell him you're looking for him," Carol interjected.

"Right, you do that."

We watched the young girl flounce away into the crowd, then Carol turned to me, and I to her.

"Well, what do you think about that?"

"There's so much wrong with what just happened, I don't know where to begin."

"I can't imagine Fredric skipping dress rehearsal," Carol huffed, "letting all those people down, no matter what was taking place in his personal life."

"I can't imagine Seleia dumping him like that," I shot back.

Carol waggled her head. "She's a redhead, dear. Bound to be adventurous. But if she thinks she's going to get anywhere with that director person, she'll be sorely disappointed."

"I agree with you there," I nodded. "Say, now that the booth is running smoothly, Mum, would you mind if I took off for a bit?"

"You're not planning to follow Seleia and sleuth around her rehearsal to see if you can pick up any information on Fredric, are you?"

"Of course not," I retorted far too vehemently since that had been exactly what I was going to do. "I just want to look at a few booths I saw yesterday before the good stuff gets sold out."

"Bring me back a maple bar from the Voodoo Donut stand, will you?"

"Sure thing," I said as I took my leave.

Though I enjoyed spending time with my mother, I felt a certain relief as I walked away into the happy, milling crowd. I liked being on my own, not having to answer to anyone or explain my reasoning for doing what I did. I could still sneak up to the auditorium—Carol would never know the difference, and besides, it was my life. But she was right—it would be an imposition. No, best to stick with plan B and see what the vendors' room had to offer.

I proceeded down the aisle toward the back of the hall. Walking slowly, I took in the wares to either side. Dried fall flower arrangements, Halloween decorations, and cookies shaped like pumpkins were in the majority, but there were also crocheted goods, pottery, handmade soaps, toys, collectibles, and pillows shaped like cartoon characters. I paused at a display of herbs grown by a man who lived up the street, then at a table selling life-sized cats made of clay. A sign on a black and white tuxie read, *Dishwasher Safe*. I had to laugh, trying to picture how I'd ever fit the foot-long reclining sculpture in my dishwasher even if I wanted to.

"It's sort of a joke," said the gaunt older man from behind the table. "But it gets people's attention."

I continued to chuckle. "It certainly got mine. So

they're not dishwasher-safe?"

"Oh, they are, but who'd want to? What it really means is they are water-safe so you can put them in your yard."

"I love that." On an impulse, I picked out an all-black one that reminded me of my own panther cats Tinkerbelle, Little, and Emilio. I was a great fan of *le chats noir* and considered them the best of luck in the old Scottish tradition instead of the dour and depressing American one.

"Can I leave it here until I'm ready to go?" I asked after paying. "I'd rather not have to cart it around with me." I hefted the substantial sculpture. "It's heavy as a real cat!"

"What? You don't want to lug a ten-pound hunk of stone around the fair with you?" His eyes twinkled as he teased. "Sure, I'll put it under the table. What's your name?"

"Lynley."

Linlee, he wrote on a post-it which he affixed to the black back. "It'll be here for you whenever you're ready."

I browsed a few more aisles, but the room was getting crowded, so I decided it was time to see what else the fête had to offer. Picking up a printed map from the table in the entrance hall, I scanned it to see where I might like to go next. I could skip the child-oriented activities and the daycare center, and I didn't feel the need of the fortune teller on the second floor. I wasn't hungry, so the food court was out, but the acapella choir performance in the penthouse sounded appealing. They weren't on until three o'clock though—I had an hour to kill.

It was fate, I told myself when I finally decided there was nothing for it but to go to the auditorium and check on the dress rehearsal. I was curious to see if Fredric had shown up, but I made a personal vow I wouldn't pry.

Slipping silently through the door, past the sign that read, "No Admittance—Rehearsal In Progress," I took a seat in the shadows at the back. It was a love scene, but instead of Fredric's familiar face in the part of Lysander, I saw a stranger. That answered my question whether he had made it or not. *Should I be worried?* I wondered to myself.

I was quickly caught up in the familiar-but-different twists of the revised plot and the superb—at least for amateurs—performance of the actors. Seleia was gorgeous in her flouncy blue costume, and the boy playing opposite, though not as charismatic as Fredric, was doing a reasonable job for a stand-in. By intermission, when I left to get Carol her donut, then run upstairs to see the choir, I'd forgotten all about the absent Fredric.

Chapter 16

Are cats psychic? Cats have the ability to sniff out danger, and in that way, basically foretell the future.

Fredric never did show up for dress rehearsal, nor did he don his sunflower costume to pass out leaflets for the play—Seleia the Bee had to do it on her own. She was not happy, as I heard in no uncertain terms when she phoned me at the ungodly hour of midnight. Though having been interrupted from my beauty sleep, I felt honored she chose to call her grandmother in her moment of woe. It made no difference that there was nothing I could say or do, that her love life was a path she would have to travel on her own, I was there for her no matter what, and she knew it. She did get me thinking though—what had become of Fredric? A young man prone to act on whim, he still knew where his responsibilities lay, and running off without a word seemed out of character.

Next morning I put on my coat and crossed the street to Fredric's duplex. His car was still parked in the same place. He really needed to move it soon or our neighbor Seamus and his kindly wife who watched over the block like a mother cat would summon the police for violation of the 48-hour law. That ticket wasn't cheap, and if the cops decided to make an example of it and have the car towed, it would cost even more.

Climbing the short flight of cement steps to the porch, I knocked and rang the bell. I doubted I'd get an answer, but I had to try. I waited a minute or two, then moved closer to peer through the little square pane. From there, I could see the tiny entranceway but that was all. Retreating back down a step, I leaned in to look through the living room window. I had to stand on my tiptoes and was immediately reminded of my adventure at the Cat House. I'd end up with a reputation as a voyeur if I didn't watch out.

I got myself balanced and scanned the room, but there was nothing to see. A relatively tidy space for a bachelor, but no Fredric. Also, no Tarzan. I supposed the kitten could be in the bedroom or bathroom, but that brought up another question—would Fredric have gone off and left the baby cat alone for days? There was no way, and a full bowl of kibble by the fireplace bore out that theory. If Tarzan were there, he would surely have made a dent in it by now.

Odd as it seemed, it looked like Fredric had taken his cat and left. To sulk about his girlfriend's mean treatment? I doubted it. Fredric had more resilience than that. A call for work? Things happened fast in the film industry, and as a production assistant he couldn't very well refuse a job. Maybe it had to do with his Aunt Grace who had raised him from childhood. She was older—had she fallen ill and needed his help? I was sure he would drop everything for her, but it didn't explain why he hadn't told someone he was leaving. Or why he hadn't taken his car.

I walked back across the street and let myself in my front door where Little was waiting for me on the cabinet. She was my welcoming committee, and though I'd been gone for less than five minutes, she made it her business to greet me with headbutts and chirps of pleasure.

I took off my coat and snuggled her into my arms.

Carrying her through to the kitchen, I let her down on the mission oak table where she turned in a circle, then stared up at me.

"I'm in a quandary," I told the black cat. "We seem to have misplaced our friend Fredric."

Purrumph, she replied solemnly.

"I know he's a capable young man," I went on, "but one worries."

Purrr, she agreed.

"And strange things are happening in our area—men are disappearing then reappearing in shocking condition. Poor Gerald Sullivan was literally at death's door."

Prrumph-rumph, Little opined.

I moved to the mug of coffee I'd left on the counter, then hesitated. "I'm sure this is nothing so dire..."

Suddenly Mab jumped up on the table beside Little. Uttering a long, ominous yowl, she stared at me with the blue-eyed intensity I had come to know well.

Mab was special, but it wasn't because she was a pedigreed lilac point Siamese. As she matured from a kitten to a cat, she began displaying powers of a psychic nature. It didn't come all at once, and at first, I passed her apt warnings off as coincidence. I'd become accustomed to Little's ability to sense when things were off, communicating with a touch of a paw or a flick of an ear, but Mab took it a step further—several steps, in fact. It was as if I could understand her thoughts, thoughts that often were premonitions of things to come.

Now Mab's psychic presence hit me like a rampaging lion. Something was wrong.

"Mab, what is it?" Though the sense of doom was tangible, there was nothing visual to accompany it. Mab's warning might have been about anything, from the state of her food bowl to the state of the world, but I had the feeling it was somewhere closer to home. "Is it Fredric? Is he in danger?"

Up until that moment, I hadn't let myself dwell on the similarities between Fredric's unexpected withdrawal and those of the I-5 Lost Boys. I couldn't. The idea was unthinkable. But with my prognosticating cat staring me in the face, eyes like vortexes into another dimension, I could think about nothing else.

Staggering under the enormity of the revelation, I sank into a chair, my coffee left forgotten on the counter. Mab stalked up to me, her face level with mine. She blinked once—not a love blink but something other—then hopped into my lap and curled up as if nothing had happened. Whatever she had wanted to convey to me was done, and now she was ready to move on to gentler things, such as a nap. For a very long time, I petted her satin fur and tried to convince myself I was mistaken.

* * *

I must have spaced out for longer than I'd imagined, because when my mother called to wish me a happy Halloween and to remind me that we were meeting for lunch before Seleia's performance, it was already after eleven. I almost told Carol about my fears for Fredric but caught myself. She sounded so perky on the phone I didn't want to bother her with my random yet disturbing supposition. Besides, with the optimism of pure denial, I convinced myself I'd got it all wrong—surely Fredric would be back for the play that afternoon.

I considered going by the Cat House. I'd dropped in the night before but stayed only for the bare minimum to make sure things were going smoothly and to pick up my pay, another suspicious pile of hundred dollar bills. The cats were fine, no moans from the demon room or calls on the old fashioned landline. I'd been in and out in half an hour, but now I felt guilty. I hadn't even tried to engage the cats in play.

To be honest, I was a bit miffed at Darla who had yet to tell me when she would be home. She seemed to think it was perfectly alright to go about her business without letting me know, but I shouldn't take it out on the cats. It wasn't their fault their person was a flake. At least she was concerned enough about their wellbeing to hire a cat sitter. When she got back from this trip, though, the two of us were going to sit down and have a serious talk.

Deciding to delay the visit until the evening when I could stay with the clowder for as long as they wanted, I went about a few chores I'd been neglecting, beginning with litter boxes. With nine cats in the house, the commodes needed constant surveillance, but beyond that was the bigger job of deep cleaning. That meant swapping out the plastic boxes themselves—lugging the used ones into the basement and blasting them with hot water and soap. It was a tedious and exhausting business, but when I was done, I felt like I'd accomplished a Herculean task.

With Halloween upon us, the festival would be going strong. Thankfully the Terrace Traders had a flock of volunteers to man their booth, so Carol could take a break which meant I could take one too. I still needed to fix bowls of candy for the night visitors. These days, most parents took their kids to safe parties and events like the ones that would be going on at the fête, but there were still a few neighbors who wanted to show off their costumes around the homes. Sometimes I even dressed up myself. I'd bring out the red Star Trek uniform, the only costume I owned, and flash the Vulcan peace sign at the kids. It was fun to join in, but this holiday I had too many other things on my mind.

After a short session on the computer answering emails, catching up with Facebook, and getting lost a few times in the whirlwind of the web, I went upstairs, put on a nice black skirt and my black cat Halloween sweater. I said goodbye to the kitties who were mostly napping and took off to meet Carol at the Pub and Pony.

I'd asked Frannie to join us, and when I arrived, there she was with my mum and Candy, saving me a place at the big window table.

"You're late," admonished Carol.

"I'm not," I countered—this was a running theme with us. "You're early."

"Frannie's on time," Carol said as if she hadn't heard me. "Why can't you be more like your friend?"

I sat in the vacant chair. "Alright, you win. Next time we'll be sure to synchronize our watches before we meet."

"But Lynley, you don't wear a watch," Candy observed. "You tell time on your phone."

"And...?" I laughed.

"Oh, I get it—cell phone time synchronizes itself."

"Exactly."

Carol harrumphed. "I was just about to catch Frannie up on the saga of Seleia's love life. Did she call you last night?"

I nodded. "At midnight."

"Us too," Candy sighed. "She's really angry with Fredric for running off without telling her."

"That's the nature of young love," Carol mused. "All ups and downs. Why, I remember my first love." She gave a wistful smile. Dare I say her eyes got misty? "He was fifteen and I was fourteen. He'd walk me home from school by way of the river. One day, he..."

"That's enough, Mum. We have more important things to think about."

"Like what?" Carol defended.

"Like..." My thoughts took an unwanted turn to the missing Fredric. I quashed them and said instead," Seleia's play. Frannie, are you joining us? I sat in on a bit of the dress rehearsal yesterday, and it looks like it's going to be good."

"It's a parody," Carol commented. "Not the real Midsummer Night's Dream."

"Lynley told me," said Frannie. "I've heard of the writer, Kiefer Clark. He's quite well-known in local theater. It should be interesting if nothing else."

"They're lucky to have him," I added. "He's locally famous, but I gather one of his favorite things, beyond writing and directing, is introducing young people to the dramatic arts. He certainly has made an impression on Seleia."

"She's considering switching her major to drama." Carol frowned. "I don't know what to think about that. Theater is fun—I should know having dabbled myself—but it's cutthroat when it comes to acting as a career. I wouldn't wish that on our girl."

"I hope she doesn't make any rash decisions," said Frannie. "Kids her age see only the glamour, not all the obstacles that they'll have to face."

"Thank goodness," I responded. "If they really knew how hard it is to make it in today's society, they'd never bother to get out of bed."

Candy gave a little gasp. "Oh, you can't believe that, Lynley. Life is wonderful at any stage, if only you can find your light."

I sighed. "You're right. But I wouldn't go back to that blissful but blind naïveté, even if I were paid."

Carol gave me a sour look. "What's the matter, dear? You're unusually cynical this morning. Is it that crazy cat sitting job again?"

"No, not really, though I do wish Darla was better at communicating. I still don't know when she plans to be back. No, it's just... well..." *Not Fredric... Not Fredric...* "maybe it's the time of year. Seasonal depression or some such."

"Has your anxiety disorder been flaring up again?"

"It's a lot of things," I replied elusively. "Special Agent Paris took me on an investigation into a hoarding situation. I felt so sorry for the woman—she'd just let things get out of hand. NHS is going to help her with the cats, but it's sad all the way around. And then this thing with Fredric and Seleia. I know I can't do anything about it, but I like Fredric. I'd really hate to see them split up. But let's talk about something else, like what we're going to order. The server keeps looking over, and we haven't even picked up our menus yet."

Everyone was ready to contemplate food instead of the weight of the universe. Without argument, we opened our menus and began to peruse.

"Is Seleia's mom coming to see the play?" Frannie asked me after putting in her order for a vegan Cobb salad.

The mention of Lisa hit me like cold water on a cat. Though I loved my daughter, we had issues.

"She and Gene are at their L.A. place for the month," I said stiffly. "She was going to fly back for the show, but something came up."

I pursed my lips and bit my tongue—so many things

were wrong with that statement. How could anything be more important than Seleia's first play? But that was my daughter through and through, a woman totally consumed with herself.

Lisa Cannon Voxx was a running dichotomy in my head and heart. As she'd grown up, her lifestyle and beliefs veered further and further from mine. Her need to climb the social ladder was part of her persona as an artist, and she used those superficial connections to promote and sell her work. I did my best to accept it, but she refused to reciprocate, never missing a chance to berate me for being the vintage hippie and cat woman that I was. Our meetings too often devolved into criticism and arguments. For Seleia's sake, I tried to take whatever Lisa hurled at me like a lady, but a better tactic was to avoid those confrontations altogether.

To that end, I couldn't help feeling a little relieved Lisa wasn't coming today so I didn't have to listen to her account of everything that was wrong with me. But I was being selfish—her presence would have meant the world to Seleia.

"Lisa has an art opening," explained Carol, coming to my rescue. "She's become quite renowned in those circles. I do know that she means to send flowers, so that should be a nice touch. And Seleia's friends from school will be there, so she'll have plenty of support."

"Do you think Fredric will make it after all?" Candy put out wistfully.

"Fredric?" Frannie frowned. "What's happened to Fredric? I thought he was playing the lead?"

Carol turned to Frannie, her face growing somber. "That's what I was about to tell you when Lynley came in. Fredric didn't merely stand Seleia up for a date—the young man seems to have fallen off the face of the Earth."

Chapter 17

Many animal advocates have chosen a vegan lifestyle. Veganism goes beyond a vegetarian diet into every aspect of one's life.

Lunch at the Pub and Pony was excellent—a vegan mushroom burger with all the fresh trimmings for me, and various assorted savories, both vegetarian and non-veg for Frannie, Carol, and Candy. When we'd finished, we piled into Frannie's Prius, and she shuttled us the ten blocks down to the Masonic Hall. We talked of many things but never touched back on Fredric's absence. Yet Carol's worrying words echoed in my head—*Fredric's fallen off the face of the Earth*. Was that true? And if so, what did it mean?

Since there was nothing I could do about it besides fret, I made the resolution to put all grim possibilities aside for the next hour and see what happened. Maybe someone in the cast would have heard from him. Maybe he would miraculously appear. And if he didn't, I could worry then.

I'd watched the busy set crew decorating the theater hall at dress rehearsal yesterday, but walking into the full effect of their work left me speechless. I don't think I'd ever seen so many fairy lights in one place in my life. In a range of fall colors— reds, yellows, greens, and amber— they lit the old hall with a million twinkles that reflected off the golden moldings and the brass fitted chairs. The stage itself was ringed with the tiny lights along with strings of round white globes and tiny Chinese lanterns, giving the impression of a vignette. The resulting ambiance was mystical and not quite real—a fey realm, perfect for an autumn night's dream.

The old burgundy velvet curtains were drawn, but I could see a slight ripple as the cast hustled about making last minute set changes and getting to their marks.

"Lynley, over here!" A young woman in the front row was standing and waving. I recognized her as one of Seleia's college friends—Patsy? Penny? "We saved a seat for you."

"I'm Penelope," she said as we joined her up front. "And this is Kevin, Ronin, and Cey," she added, introducing her cohorts. "Seleia wasn't sure how many there would be, so she told us to save the whole row."

I raised an eyebrow, wondering what sort of pull my dear granddaughter had to reserve the entire first row but put it aside, thankful for the favor. "It's just us—Seleia's great grandmother Carol, her friend Candy, and my friend Frannie."

"Her mom and dad didn't make it?" Penelope frowned.

"I'm sorry to say, no." Carol grimaced. "But she knew that, didn't she?"

"Yeah, but you know how it is. She was still hoping they might have a last minute change of heart."

"I'm sure they would be here if they could," I mumbled.

"Well, maybe they can make the encore," Penelope said hopefully. I took an immediate liking to this girl who seemed to care about her friend's wellbeing.

"Encore?" Carol asked. "This is the first I've heard about an encore."

"Yeah," the boy Ronin piped up. He swept a great lock

of bleached hair out of his face. "Kiefer decided the show was too good to only do once and got a gig with the Arts Alliance for the weekend before Thanksgiving."

"Nice," I commented. "Maybe her parents can make it then."

"And maybe by then Delarosa will have remembered he's part of the cast," Cey sighed. "Finn makes an okay Lysander, but his Puck leaves a lot to be desired. Fredric is way better."

"Then he's still missing?" I stuttered.

"No one's heard a thing," said Penelope. "He's either the biggest jerk on Earth..." She paused. "Or something's wrong."

"Like what?" I found myself saying, though images were already forming in my mind—again.

But if Penelope had any insight as to what may have befallen Fredric, it was fated to go unsaid. The house lights dimmed, and a rumble of loud voices could be heard entering the theater through both outer doors. Down the aisles rushed the cast, all talking at the top of their lungs. Some were dressed in normal street clothes while others were costumed in Shakespearian splendor. I caught sight of Seleia in the gorgeous blue dress with the sequined bodice. Among the autumn colors, she stood out like a sapphire.

The actors rushed the stage, still laughing and talking among themselves. They pushed up the steps and exited into the wings. The talking continued from offsides, gaining in volume; then all at once, it stopped, leaving an echo in the silence.

From the shadows, one man appeared. He walked slowly, eyes cast to the floor, stopping when he reached center stage. Wearing the exact same color suit as the curtain behind him, he seemed like a disembodied head. The head rose, looking the audience in the eye—Kiefer Clark himself—as he made the grand introduction.

"'I have had the most rare vision. I had a dream, past the wit of a human to say what dream it was... The eye of a human hath not heard, the ear of a human hath not seen, a human's hand is not able to taste, their tongue to conceive, nor their heart to report, what my dream was...'"

* * *

The play was entrancing, carrying the audience, me included, into a place of fanciful make-believe. Though it basically followed the great bard's masterpiece, Clark had taken liberties with both plot and characters to make it relevant to autumn. He had also condensed it from a five-act play to two with a short intermission in between.

Act one had gone well apart from poor Finn, the understudy for Lysander and Puck. As hard as he tried to fill Fredric's ballet slippers, the lack of rehearsal showed. He stumbled on lines multiple times, and twice, he forgot them entirely and had to be prompted. At one point, Seleia took over, ad-libbing his part as well as her own. She did it magnificently, and with all the alterations Clark had made to the play, few in the audience knew the difference. The only reason I picked up on it was that she had mentioned the scene, how it was her favorite, and how Fredric could make the words come alive.

The moment the curtain fell for intermission, Seleia's friends ran off in a fit of giggles. Frannie left to make a phone call. Carol and Candy went to get drinks and invited me along, but I decided to remain in my seat, not feeling like braving the crush of theatergoers heading for the bar and the restrooms.

Now alone in the front row, I felt my phone buzz, a text from Seleia.

Plz come to stage left I need to talk 2 U

I looked up to see her beckoning from the shadows. Leaving my coat on the chair, I walked over to the stairs at the side of the stage.

"Come on up," she whispered hurriedly. No sooner had I made the top step, she grabbed my arm and pulled me into the wings. Before I could ask what was wrong, she burst into tears.

I put my arms around her. "What is it? What's happened?"

She took a deep breath and forced the crying to stop. Her makeup had already begun to run—she would have to touch it up before the next act.

"Oh, Grandmother, it's terrible. Everything's so messed up. Finn is awful as Lysander and even worse as Puck. He's ruining the play, and it's all my fault."

"Why would you say that?"

"I'm the reason Fredric ran out on us." She blinked back the tears that were threatening to start up again. "If I hadn't broken up with him, he'd be here."

"You don't know that, love. He could have left for some other reason entirely."

This didn't seem to register with her, as she continued to lament. "My big opportunity is turning into a total flop!"

"That's not true. The play's going really well. Everybody loves it. And if you're talking about your little improvisation back there, I don't think anyone noticed. It's not like you're going by Shakespeare's original script."

She blinked at me questioningly. "Really? It's not dreadful?"

"Far from it. Didn't you hear the applause?"

"Yes, but I figured since most of the audience is related to someone in the cast, they'd have to clap no matter what."

"Well, I could see their faces. Family or not, they're loving it. Now you go back and get yourself fixed up for the next act. And don't worry. The show must go on, you know."

I smiled, and so did Seleia.

She gave me a quick hug. "I love you, Lynley."

"Me, too, sweetie. See you after the show."

A few minutes later, the house lights flashed, and people began to retake their seats. Another minute and we were again plunged into the radiant dark. Clark repeated his stage walk, with an intro to act two, and we were off on the adventure that only live theater can provide.

Seleia had wholeheartedly resumed her part and was stellar at it. Carol kept nudging me proudly every time she came on, to the point I finally had to tell her to knock it off. Finn's performance may not have been flawless, but it was much improved—he must have spent intermission going over his lines. The twists and turns of the play itself—mostly courtesy of the original playwright but with innovations by the talented Kiefer Clark—kept the audience on their toes, hanging on every line, immersed until the final curtain.

As the actors came back for their bows, the theater went wild. Everyone stood and clapped and hooted. Flowers and sprigs of autumn leaves were tossed upon the stage. An older woman—meaning thirties in contrast to the twenty-something cast—walked on carrying a bundle of roses so large it nearly obscured her gray satin dress. Smiling proudly, she crossed to Seleia, and with great flamboyance, passed her the bouquet. Seleia's surprise and pleasure were tangible, and when the woman whispered something in her ear, she burst into tears, but this time they were happy ones. She gave a little bow, and the curtain came down once more.

The delivery of the bouquet and the candid response from Seleia had touched the hearts of the audience, and instead of diminishing, the ovation grew louder. A second curtain call revealed the entirety of the cast with Seleia and Clark positioned in the center. The group gave an amazingly synchronized bow, then began laughing and talking loudly. They bustled off stage, down the steps, and out through the aisles the way they had come. As Seleia passed, I caught her eye and winked. I couldn't see if she winked back, but she was grinning from ear to ear.

Once the actors were gone, the hubbub died down, and people began to gather their things. When I turned to Penelope, I saw she was crying.

"That was so wonderful!" she gasped. "I'm so glad to see Seleia finding herself like that. And to think, she was about to waste her life as a scientist!"

I didn't agree that a career as a particle physicist was a wasted life, but Penelope was right about the fact that Seleia clearly loved acting. She had simply glowed. Whether this appreciation of the dramatic arts would be sustainable as a vocation was yet to be seen. It didn't matter—Seleia had her life ahead of her. Besides, who said an actor couldn't be a physicist as well?

"We're heading up to the cast party," said Penelope. "Are you and your friends coming too?"

"Cast party?" I remarked. "I haven't been invited."

"Anyone can come. It's just upstairs in the green room. You should go. It'll be fun."

"Okay. Thanks for letting me know."

I watched her and her group make their way into the crowd and depart up the aisle.

"Cast party," I mumbled to Carol. "Did you know about that?"

"Of course." Carol collected her coat and purse. "Seleia asked us specially."

"She didn't say anything to me," I pouted.

"That's because I was supposed to tell you. Sorry, dear, I forgot. But no matter. I'm telling you now."

I looked at my phone—it was already getting late. "I've got cat sitting tonight. I really should go home." I turned to Frannie. "But it's up to you since you're my ride."

"I've never been to a cast party before, and it sounds like fun, but I can take you home first if that's what you'd rather."

"Would you mind? The trick-or-treaters will be out soon, and after that, I've got to feed my cats."

"Then it's settled," said Carol. "See you in the green room when you get back, Frannie. Goodnight Lynley." She leaned over and gave my hand a squeeze. "You take this cat sitting job too seriously for my way of thinking, but it's your life, dear. Take care."

"I will. Goodnight, Mum, Candy. Give Seleia my love."

Night was already closing in as Frannie and I left the building, and a fog had fallen, giving the streetlights and neon signs an eerie glow. Among the usual street folk were demons, ghosts, superheroes, and butterflies—kids out for Halloween. One mini-ghoul was clad in a particularly disturbing outfit, a strip of blue tarp much like the one worn by the kidnap victim Gerald Sullivan before he died. But as the boy moved closer, I saw I was mistaken. Not a tarp at all but a blue cape—a Batman.

I lowered my eyes to the foggy sidewalk and walked the rest of the way to Frannie's car without looking up again.

Chapter 18

Those gauzy fake cobwebs that people spread around home and garden on Halloween pose a danger to wildlife. Birds and insects are especially vulnerable if the webs are hung in their flightpath.

Maybe it was the weather, the foreboding fog that swirled through the streets and across the lawns. Maybe it was the letdown of being on my own after the excitement and pleasure of time spent with friends and family. Maybe it was the innate dynamics of Halloween, now a holiday for children, but once a night of pagan power. I couldn't put a finger on it, but I felt ill at ease.

I dared not turn on the overhead lights until I was ready to greet the little tricksters with my bowl full of candy bribes, so I moved around the house, shedding my coat, putting away my purse, petting the cats who were starting to think of dinnertime, in relative darkness. Slipping into the kitchen, I switched on a table lamp, hoping that bit of glow wouldn't alert the hoard, then I brewed a cup of genmaicha for a bit of a lift. I would have preferred chamomile and a short nap, but it wasn't the plan. Tonight's plan had me up and running for hours to come.

I tossed a handful of dry treats on the floor for the clowder. "That's got to hold you until the children have come and gone," I told them stubbornly. Hermione, the newcomer to my clowder, answered with a querulous *wowww*, but the others just tucked into the kibble, thankful for what they got.

Pulling a wooden bowl from the cupboard, I grabbed the bags of individually wrapped candy bars that were stashed on the kitchen counter. Tearing open one of the bags, I frowned. At one time, it would have been little boxes of raisins, a healthier treat, but after hearing how kids tossed anything not dripping with chocolate, I'd finally bowed to custom. *Let the little rascals binge their hearts out.* They weren't my kids, and I didn't have to deal with their sugar rush or listen to their groans when their tummies ached.

When did I get so cynical? I suddenly wondered. My mother had mentioned it earlier. A certain amount of healthy skepticism, yes, but this downright *to heck with everything* wasn't like me. More concerning even was the fact I didn't know where it was coming from.

I took my tea into the living room and sat down on the couch. Picking up Dirty Harry who was curled on the cushion, I placed him on my lap. He blinked questioningly, but his query was simple: "Why have you woken me?"

I leaned over and buried my face in his fur, breathing in the sweet cat smell of him. I loved that smell—it always calmed me, and this was no exception.

Harry gave a sigh and tucked his head back down. The old cat enjoyed his lap-naps these days. When he was younger and busy mousing, prowling, and playing, the only time he would settle on a human was when he was wet and cold. He would come in from the rainy outdoors and make a beeline onto my nice absorbent clothing where his fur would dry, and I'd end up sopping. As time went by, he became more sedentary, and I enjoyed his weighty warmth as I watched television or worked on the computer. I was enjoying it now, sipping my tea in the dark and letting my mind wander.

The ring of the doorbell shocked me out of my comfortable contemplation. Annoyed by my inadvertent jerk, Harry leapt away and stalked into the kitchen to see if he could find a kibble treat the others had missed.

Rats! I swore to myself as I jumped into action, heading for the bowl of candy. As I rushed to the door, I couldn't help but wonder what bold child would have the audacity—and the fearlessness—to approach an unlit porch.

Flinging open the door and proffering the bowl, I found it wasn't a child at all.

"Lynley?" The slim woman had been about to head back down the steps but now she turned, my neighbor Patty. "I didn't think you were home. All your lights were off."

"Patty! Oh, I'm glad it's you. I wasn't quite ready for the Halloween onslaught, so I was keeping it dark. But I guess I'm ready now."

I set the bowl on the side table and clicked on the porch light, noticing Patty had something in her hand.

She held out a flat box wrapped in orange tissue paper and tied with a black bow. "This is for you. It's a little thank you."

"For what?" I took the box. The big gold sticker on the ribbon branded it as chocolates from Zeno's, my favorite local chocolatier.

"For being a great neighbor," Patty replied. "For all the good works you do taking care of cats at your shelter. For introducing Jim and me to Kitty, the love of our lives." She gave a slightly embarrassed shrug. "If you hadn't encouraged us to adopt her, we might never have known how wonderfully she completes our family."

"Wow! This is a surprise!" I took another look at the unexpected gift, then at Patty. In her early thirties, she could easily masquerade as someone much younger. Her stature, only a little over five feet, added to the pixie effect, as did her cute brown bob and wide, amber eyes. "Would you like to come in?"

"No, I'd better get home. As you said, the kids will be out any minute, and I shouldn't leave Jim to face them by himself. We put Kitty in her room so she wouldn't get excited by the callers. She's a black cat so we're taking every precaution."

"I need to corral my clowder as well. They're pretty good about visitors, but…"

"Kids can be noisy and excitable. They can scare a cat without meaning to."

I held up the candy box. "Thank you for this, Patty. You really made my day. But, if I may ask, why now? Out of the blue like this?"

Patty shook her head, sending her hair bouncing. "It's a group I joined, the Gratitude Group. We get together once a week on Zoom and talk about things we're thankful for. It's supposed to help people concentrate on the positive things that happen to them instead of just the negative. We're encouraged to thank the people in our lives who help us or inspire us. And Lynley, you've definitely done that for me."

I felt my face flush, but in a good way. "That sounds like a great group. You should send me the link. I could use some positivity in my life right now."

"Why? Is something wrong?"

I peered past her, across the street to Fredric's duplex. Still dark as a black cat. "No, not really. I don't know…"

I was about to ask if by chance Patty had seen any sign of Fredric when a scream split the night. There was another and another, then giggles. The trick-or-treaters were on their way.

"Oh-oh, here they come. I'd better run."

"Thanks again, Patty," I called as she sprang down the steps. "Drop by for tea and help me eat these delicacies before I devour the whole box myself."

She turned and waved. "Will do. Talk soon."

With that, she was gone to the apartments next door. From the opposite direction came the kids, at least half a dozen of them along with a pair of adults trying to look inconspicuous and failing. As the entourage approached, rushing each house with innocent enthusiasm, I quickly went to herd the cats.

* * *

The kids were cute in their fancy costumes, and I found myself getting into the mood. The mist no longer spooked me, instead merely adding to the Halloween ambiance. I had no porch decorations, but others on the block did, including Seamus across the street, who went all out with twinkly orange lights and a blowup ghost family on the lawn. No one on our block used those fake spiderwebs after I led a campaign against them, educating folks on the dangers they presented to birds and animals.

There were five groups of children over the next hour, all of whom I recognized from the neighborhood. By far the cutest, in my totally biased opinion, was a tiny kitty princess who couldn't have been more than four years old. As soon as I opened the door, she peered past me into the hallway. Instead of the usual *trick or treat*, she asked, "Are you the cat lady?"

I smiled and said, "Why, yes, I am."

Then she ran forward and hugged my knees. "I love cats!" she exclaimed into my skirt.

The oldest kids were a pair of boys of around fourteen. One was dressed as a rock star and the other as a pirate. I knew some folks balked at the older trick-or-treaters, but to me they were precious. Only last year or the year before, they had been children—now they were faced with coming of age. I wasn't going to thwart their final throwback to innocence. Besides, I knew these boys, and they were good kids. I would do what I could to help them stay that way.

Finally the visits petered out, the sounds of laughter growing dim and then ceasing altogether. I put the candy bowl, now much diminished, on the side table, clicked off the porch light, and grabbing a candy for myself, went to let the cats out. They emerged from the back rooms meowing with anticipation, certain that finally it was time to eat.

"You're right, kitties," I told them, sinking onto the couch and ripping the wrapper off the tiny chocolate bar. "Give me a moment to recuperate, and dinner will be served."

The sweet chocolate and caramel melted in my mouth, giving me a much needed boost of sugar energy. I thought about the box of gourmet chocolates Patty had brought me—I'd save that special treat for a later time when we could enjoy the little delights together. What a lovely idea, acknowledging gratitude every day, then carrying it one step further to show appreciation to those in our lives who had done something special. I wasn't sure I deserved it—I was no hero. Still, if everyday kindness counted, I did my best to fill that role.

Emilio hopped into my lap, fifteen pounds of black floof, and proceeded to argue that I was in fact not fulfilling my most important role, that of meal provider. He wasn't alone—Big Red jumped up beside me, and Mab let go a Siamese wail from the kitchen. My moment of rest was over.

* * *

Just as I finished dishing out the last of the wet food and Violet's diet dry, my phone rang.

"Hello, Seleia. How are you?" Though seemingly innocuous, it was a loaded question, and I didn't know what to expect. The play had ended fabulously, but the last time I'd talked with my granddaughter, she was beside herself. Knowing Seleia, it could now go either way.

"I'm brilliant!" she announced. "I just wanted to give you a call to tell you how much I appreciated you being there for me this afternoon. I was pretty miserable during intermission—what you said meant a lot."

Topping up my tea with boiling water from the instant tap, I took both phone and tea to the loveseat by the window where I collapsed with a sigh.

"Thank you, love. And the play was excellent—your performance especially, of course."

Seleia chuckled. "You have to say that, Grandmother."

"No, I don't. I have to be supportive of you, no matter what, but I'd never lie to you."

"Well, it was really fun, and I did love doing it. And…" she began tentatively, "I want to do it more. What do you think?"

"I suppose that depends on what you mean by doing more," I replied carefully. I had my opinions, but this was about her, and I needed to keep an open mind. "Having a go at a few more amateur productions is one thing, where devoting your life to the theater would be another."

"And what if I did? Devoted my life to drama, or at least the next three years?"

"You're considering changing your major from science to dramatic arts?"

A pause. "I am."

There was another pause, then the dam broke, and she began to gush.

"Oh, Lynley," she began, using my first name as she tended to do when she wanted to speak adult to adult, "I feel it! I feel it in my soul. I know this was just a little play, but I learned so much! And I was good at it—Kiefer said so. And he's going to help me choose my classes—he teaches some of them himself. Most are for advanced students, but he says when I complete the basics, he'll get me in. It's a once-in-a-lifetime opportunity. I'd be silly not to take it."

So there it was. Kiefer Clark, Seleia's crush. I had to say something—it was my duty as a grandmother—but I would need to use tact or this young woman who was still part little girl would get her fur up and run the other way.

"You know I believe in you…"

I heard an "Mmmm…" on the line—she knew what was coming.

"And I will support whatever decision you make. You can do anything you set your mind to—I truly believe that. But I want you to ask yourself one question before you decide to quit your scientific studies."

"Alright…" she said warily. "What's that?"

The crunch. I hate the crunch. If it worked, fine, but if it backfired, things could fall apart fast. "Are you doing this because you love drama or because you like Kiefer Clark?"

For a moment, there was silence, then I heard a strange, muffled sound. Had I stepped over the line? Had I made her cry?

The sound rose in volume, and I realized it wasn't a sob but laughter, muffled because she was trying to contain it and couldn't.

"Oh, Grandmother," she gasped between guffaws. "Did you think there was something going on between Kiefer and me?" Again she broke down. *Doth the lady protest too much?* I wondered. But then she sobered enough to speak plainly. "I do feel an affinity with Kiefer, and that's probably the vibe you got. Okay, yes, I was a little enamored with him at the beginning, but who wouldn't be? He's such a... such a talented, vivacious person. But he's married."

That wasn't the information I'd expected, and all I could say was, "Oh?"

"Yes, he brought his spouse to the cast party—his *husband*, George."

Again, all I could think to say was, "Oh."

Thankfully, Seleia went on. "No, Lynley, I assure you, this is my own personal decision, and I feel in my heart it's the right one."

She paused. "We can talk about it further if you disagree."

"I'd like to talk more, dear, but I don't disagree." I exhaled. "In fact, I think it's sort of wonderful. You're so good at anything you love. You may not become a movie star, but I know you'll shine bright."

"What? You don't think I'll be the next Emma Watson?" she teased.

"Didn't Miss Watson begin acting as a child?" I shot back.

"I can play younger. At least I think I can. I guess the point is, I want to find out. And I'm not going to quit my science classes, just shift my major. If I work hard, I can graduate with a degree in both."

"Yes, you can." I sighed—this was all good news.

"Now I've got to run, Lynley. There's a cast party after-party, and I don't want to miss it. Oh, I forgot, Granna asked me to tell you she'd got volunteers to tear down the Terrace Traders booth when it closes tonight, so you needn't worry about coming."

I gave a harrumph. "That's nice of her, since I'd already told her I was busy, and she'd have to find someone else."

Seleia laughed. "I'm staying out of this one. Talk tomorrow?"

"Sure. Have fun at your party, love."

Then we clicked off, and as my talented granddaughter set out for her first cast party after-party, I got ready to go to the Cat House.

Chapter 19

Cats can make a number of distinctively different vocalizations, both with their mouths open and closed. We learn to recognize our own cat's distinctive "voice."

The moment I walked in Darla's door, I felt something was off. The light on the end table was switched on, and the room temperature was warmer than usual. The most telling difference, however, was the cats. On previous visits, most all of them had been asleep—tonight every one was awake and prowling.

"What's up, kitties?" I asked as I hung my coat on the artsy rack. Slinging my tote onto the couch, I paused to listen. There again, something was not right.

A buzz, or possibly a hum. Perhaps a drone. Coming from somewhere inside the house. Was that what had got the cats so flustered? Though unobtrusive and benign, it was a sound I'd never heard before.

Had one of the cats managed to turn on the kitchen faucet? Or was it a radio with its dial stuck between stations that had suddenly sprung to life? The furnace? The wind in the eaves? The strange cat in the back room creating a whole new level of Siamese noises? When my imagination began running wild, contemplating ghosts and yes, demons, I decided it was time to find the source.

Yet still I stood, straining my ears for more information. Was it dangerous or nothing at all? I was on high alert, using all my senses to figure it out, but the sound eluded me.

Something brushed my leg, and I jumped like a cat, but it was only Oscar, come to see what I was doing since I was obviously not paying attention to him. I reached down and scritched his black scruff.

"Time to investigate?" I inquired.

He walked a few steps into the room, then looked back at me.

Taking that as a yes, I grabbed my phone out of my tote. I wasn't exactly scared—just wary. In my own home, I knew every single sound—this one was different from all of them. Who knew what the enigmatic Darla might have going on?

Oscar first led me into the kitchen. The faucets were off, and not even a drip fell in the granite sink. Then the refrigerator motor started up. Its noisy rumble obscured the other, softer sound, and I was again left wondering.

Turning in a circle, I tried to tune out the fridge and concentrate on the hum that lay beneath it. It seemed to be coming from the bedrooms.

Oscar had turned down the hallway. Cautiously I tiptoed behind. As I passed Darla's bedroom, Newberry rushed forward, bidding me to come play with her. I knew she must be lonely, but she was going to have to wait a few more minutes. I bent and touched the screen, telling her I'd be right back. She pushed her head against my hand, then withdrew a few feet and stood staring at me. Her mouth was slightly open, but she remained silent.

The whirr of the fridge motor clicked off, and there, nearer to the source, it became clear what I'd been hearing. Voices. Voices in the demon room.

I stopped and listened, a woman, presumably Darla—I hadn't seen her car in the driveway, but it could be in the garage—and a man. Their dialog was getting louder, as if they were arguing. I couldn't make out the words, but I was pretty sure they wouldn't want me listening in.

Quickly I retreated down the hallway. Just as I ducked around the corner, the latch clicked and the door opened.

"I gave you what you asked for, but it doesn't come cheap," the man was saying. "You know that, Dee."

"I know it," Darla retorted, "but I don't have the money. You'll have to wait until I get paid."

"Okay, I can hold off a few days longer, but you'll need to pay up before I can let you have the drugs."

Oh, my gosh! I recognized that voice—the man who'd left the message on Darla's old fashioned answering machine.

"No, please, Mickey. I need them now. I've already missed a dose. Any more slipups could delay her recovery or even cause a relapse."

There was a pause, then the man sighed. "Tell you what. Here's another day's worth, but you gotta pay me tomorrow for the rest. I'm putting myself out on a limb with this, and you know it."

"Thank you, Mickey! I'll have your money tomorrow night, I promise."

I'd been a hippie in the sixties and knew a drug deal when I heard it. I also knew that dealers disliked being observed in their dealing. It was time for me to skedaddle. Darla was home—there was no reason for me to be there at all.

It would have been nice if she had called to let me know she was back, I fumed. *Then I wouldn't be in this predicament.* Cat sitting had not turned out to be the easy, fun job I'd envisioned—not when there were drugs involved.

The clomp of footsteps coming down the hallway

broke into my angry musing. I really should have been grabbing my things and getting out of there instead of just thinking about it, because now it was too late.

Then the footsteps stopped at what I presumed to be Newberry's screen. I heard Darla croon loving words to the cat inside. Maybe I could slip away after all.

Turning, I made for the door, but as I passed the dining table, my foot caught on something, and I stumbled. Whatever I'd hit made an awful clunk and rattle, followed by the wail of a cat.

I stifled a cry, but I needn't have bothered. Darla and her cohort were on me in a heartbeat.

Darla stopped dead. "Lynley? What are you doing here?"

I stared at her, then shifted my gaze to the man looming behind her in the shadows. I knew whatever I said next could mean life or death. I decided to start with a good offense.

"Darla," I snapped back. "I didn't expect you home yet. You should have called me."

The attack seemed to work because she lowered her eyes. "Right. My bad. I meant to, then Mickey came by— Dr. Shaffer. Mickey, this is Lynley, my cat sitter."

The evil drug dealer stepped out of the shadows, morphing into a lanky, white-haired man in a nice suit and a tie. I don't think I'd ever seen anyone who looked less like a pusher.

Dr. Shaffer gave a guileless smile. "Pleased to meet you, Lynley."

My ingrained politeness took over, and I found myself mumbling, "You too—doctor?"

"Michael Shaffer, veterinarian—retired." He turned to Darla. "I'm going to take off, Dee. Remember what we talked about. If it were my call, I'd give you all the time in the world to pay—you're doing such a great job with her—but it's not up to me. They won't send the shipment until they get their money."

"I know, Mickey. I'll have it. I don't want you to jeopardize your connections. What you're doing is so important, we can't let it falter now."

Dr. Shaffer gave me a nod, handed Darla a package from out of his coat pocket, then took his leave. I turned to Darla with a head full of questions.

The woman put the box on the table and shrugged off her black cape to reveal a bright red dress with white cats appliquéd on it. "I just got in. I'm sorry I didn't text you. I didn't think I'd be back so early, but my appointment in Seattle took less time than I'd imagined. I'll still pay you for the visit. How has it been with my babies?"

"Uh, fine." I was trying to absorb what had just happened. Darla didn't seem at all hostile, so I decided to dive in. "But if you don't mind my asking, what the heck is going on here?"

Darla moved into the kitchen, flicked on the light, and retrieved a jar of loose-leaf tea. "What do you mean?"

"I couldn't help but overhear... You and Dr. Shaffer... You were talking about drugs..."

She scooped a handful of leaves into a mesh tea ball and placed it in a yellow Danish pot. Filling the pot with water from a hot-water dispenser by the sink, she turned.

"Tea? It's Darjeeling."

This threw me off. Was it a ploy, a distraction, or was she really that spacy? From my experience with her so far, I could imagine she was.

Okay, I'll play. "Yes, thank you. But first answer my question. Is that man selling you drugs?"

"Drugs?" Darla turned and broke out in laughter. "Yes, Lynley. You caught us. Dr. Shaffer is brokering illegal drugs. It's true!" she blurted to the shocked look on my face. "Or at least it sort of is."

She brought the steaming tea pot to the bar between the kitchen and the dining area. Going to the cabinet, she retrieved two Japanese porcelain cups shaped like cats.

"Come, sit, Lynley."

I seated myself tenuously on the wooden barstool. "I'm listening."

"Do you know what FIP is?" she asked quietly. "Feline Infectious Peritonitis?"

"Yes, of course. The feline coronavirus that's nearly always fatal for cats. They're working on a cure, but the medication hasn't been approved for use in the U.S. I guess some people can buy it on the black market... Wait—are you telling me you've got it?"

She shrugged. "Like I said, illegal drugs. Mickey and I are treating Sheba, the kitten in the back room."

I gasped, suddenly fascinated. As a cat person I knew of the terrible disease and the research being done to find a potential cure. FDA approval had hit a political snag, but some other countries weren't so biased, and people with afflicted kittens and cats had learned how to order it from them. An expensive pursuit with a long regimen. To undertake the treatment of a FIP cat required a hero, a wealthy one.

Darla deftly poured the tea into the delicate cups, then pushed one toward me. I took it in my hands. The hot, silky feel of the glaze brought me back to my senses.

"Is she responding?"

"Too soon to tell, but she's not getting any worse, and that's a good sign."

"That's amazing! I'm sorry, I got it all wrong. But it sounded like, well, like something very different than saving the life of a cat. May I see her?"

Darla hesitated, then said, "I guess it's okay. But you can't touch her. Don't be shocked if she looks yellow. The little dear is being treated for ringworm as well."

"Sulfur dips? Oh, poor baby! What a way to begin your life."

As I turned to rise, I again caught my foot on the thing on the floor which I now saw was a small plastic cat carrier. Suddenly I recalled the wail I'd heard the first time I kicked it.

"Hold up a minute, Darla." I picked up the carrier and peeked inside. "What's this?"

"Drat!" She came over and took the carrier from my hands. "I forgot all about this little one. Mickey was here when the Uber dropped me off, and I got totally distracted."

"You have another cat?" I huffed.

"I know, I know. I never meant to have this many, but stuff happens."

"Darla," I said as calmly as I could. "Is this a problem? Because if it is, I know people who can help. My friend Denny can come talk to you. Sometimes rescue gets out of hand." I thought of Judy Smith and the gross and unhealthy results of her well-meaning rescue attempts. "Denny is…" I paused, not wanting to come right out and label him as an animal cop who handles hoarding cases for the Northwest Humane Society, so I kept it light. "Denny's an expert on these sorts of things."

Darla wasn't listening. Instead, she had the carrier on the table and was gently teasing the cat inside. The cat gave a little *mip*.

I stiffened. I'd heard that sound before.

Darla popped the gate, and out hopped a small gray tabby. He *mipped* again, then without warning, catapulted onto my shoulder and snuggled into my hair.

Slowly, as if stunned, I pulled the kit away and held him up before me. "Tarzan?"

He blinked his big kitten eyes. "*Mip*," he purred back.

Chapter 20

Cat theft is more common than we would like to think. It is usually unplanned with the goal of profit for the thief, but sometimes thieves pick up a cat on a whim. Keeping cats indoors or in an enclosure is the best way to ensure this doesn't happen.

"What are you doing with my neighbor's cat?" I pulled Tarzan's little kitten body close and held him tightly.

Darla stared at me, her eyes wide. Then they began to narrow into a squint. She took a step forward and reached for the cat.

"No!" I shouted. If I hadn't been holding Tarzan, I might have crossed my hands in front of me, as if warding off a bad spirit. In my mind, she had become one.

Fredric was missing, and Darla had Tarzan. There could be only one conclusion…

Darla *was* the I-5 Kidnapper after all!

Now I knew the truth, but she knew I knew. My active imagination flew into overdrive, picturing all sorts of dire ends to this conversation. It was time for me to get out of there and call the police.

I turned to run, but she grabbed me. She only caught the hem of my sweater, but that was enough to jerk me back and make me lose my balance. I toppled onto the couch. Tarzan was still in my clutches, but not for long. With a lithe twist, he leapt from my grip.

I thought of trying another run for the door, but it was too late. Darla moved swiftly. Hovering over me, arms outstretched, she prepared to thwart any action I might take.

We remained frozen like that for some time, me splayed out on the sofa like a defensive cat with Darla the ready attacker. The seconds ticked away as I tried to come up with a means of escape. If not by force, then by guile? But how could I beguile her when I had no clue what she was thinking?

Suddenly she began to laugh. It wasn't one of those nefarious *Mua-ha-ha* sort of laughs but a sweet little giggle. She flopped down on the couch beside me, then placed her hand gently on mine.

"Wow, Lynley, you really had me going there. What is it? A test? A prank? A TikTok challenge? Well, whatever it was, bravo. You actually scared me."

Straightening my glasses which had fallen askew in the struggle, I stared at her in bewilderment. Then I looked away—something was wrong with this picture. To my mind, a notorious serial kidnapper shouldn't be laughing it up like a sweetheart.

"Darla," I began slowly. "I need you to answer one question for me. I want you to be honest. You can tell me anything—I won't judge you. But I need to know."

"Ooookay," she inflected.

"Where did you get that kitten?"

We both instinctively turned to Tarzan who was now sitting on the dining table next to Gloria's bed as if he owned the place.

"Why, he came from the shelter," she said. "The one where my friend works."

Of all the answers she could have given, that was not it. She sounded so innocent, so sincere.

"What shelter?" I persevered.

"The Stonehenge Cat Rescue. It's in Marysville, in Washington."

"I know of it. But I don't understand. There are shelters right here in Portland if you wanted another cat. To say nothing of the fact you've already got more cats than a hoarder—why ever would you shop for another one?"

She reddened. "I know I've got a lot of cats—but I take good care of them. You can see for yourself that I do."

"Okay, I'm sorry about the hoarder comment, but there is a limit. Everyone has a breaking point."

Darla gave a sigh. "I wasn't *shopping* for another cat, as you put it—really I wasn't. But my friend called and told me I needed to rescue him."

"Is this the same friend who got you to take Newberry last week? If so, she doesn't sound like much of a friend."

"What do you mean?"

"It seems to me she's taking advantage of your good nature," I said plainly.

"I don't know. I have wondered about it." Darla sighed once more. "I met her online through Cat Chat, and we got to talking—well, emailing. She told me how Stonehenge is a small shelter and can't meet the needs of the community. I said that was appalling and asked if there was anything I could do to help. She said maybe there was." Darla gave a little shrug. "Now whenever there's a cat they can't facilitate, she calls me to see if I'll take them." Darla hung her head. "And I do."

This revelation cast my thoughts in a whole new direction. Could Darla be so naive as to believe a shelter worker would ask a civilian to adopt their extra cats? Would a reputable shelter even do such a thing? It sounded unlikely, but if it were true, it meant Darla had nothing to do with the kidnappings after all.

Which brought me to another quandary—how a shelter in Marysville had got hold of a tabby from Portland. Had Fredric skipped out after his breakup with Seleia, just as she'd presumed? Had he taken off down the Columbia Gorge and lost Tarzan along the way? But I couldn't believe that. No matter what craziness was going on in Fredric's life, he would never have abandoned his little cat. And if Tarzan were lost, Fredric would have done everything in his power to find him, the first of which would have been to check the shelters.

What if someone had stolen Tarzan, transported him to Marysville, and let him go? But that didn't explain where Fredric himself had got off to. No, scratch both those scenarios—they were too farfetched.

"Newberry was the last one," Darla was saying, "and before that, it was Hans and Webster—no, Billy..."

I shook myself back to the present. "You've done this how many times?"

She considered. "Four. Four times before this little one. But why?"

"So, five altogether," I contemplated, then my mind began to reel. "Five cats?"

She nodded.

"You've taken five cats from your friend at the Stonehenge shelter?"

She nodded again.

"And one of them belongs to my neighbor who's gone missing..."

Suddenly the pieces fell into place, and it all made sense. I waited for Darla to make the connection. When she didn't, I pushed harder.

"Five cats, Darla. Just like the five victims of the I-5 Kidnapper, if we count my missing friend Fredric. Do you realize you may be an accessory to the abduction of five men, one of whom has died?"

Darla's face went white. "What are you talking about? I don't understand."

Her question brought me down a notch, and I began to see holes in my conclusion. Maybe I was concocting the whole scenario, adding details that weren't there. The fact was, even if this shelter worker had asked Darla to take five cats, I had no way of knowing if those cats belonged to the Lost Boys. Now that I thought about it, I realized I didn't even know if the other missing men had cats.

It was all too much. I should call the police. I'd tell them what I knew, the *only* thing I knew—that my neighbor hadn't been around for a few days and his cat had turned up at an out of town shelter. But was that enough? Would it be the clue they were looking for, or would they think I was an old lady with cats on the brain? Most likely the latter.

Meanwhile, Darla was having a little breakdown of her own. Tears rolled down her cheeks, and she huddled herself into a ball at the end of the sofa. Oscar jumped up and insinuated himself into her arms where she held him as she quietly sobbed.

"I was just trying to help," she blubbered. "I love cats. I can't stand for them to be hurt or hungry. Prin said if I didn't take them, they'd be put to sleep. What else could I do?"

She gave a whimper. "After the third one, I felt like something was amiss, but Prin just got mad when I asked about it. Lynley, I don't know what's happening. You've got to believe me."

Usually when someone says I have to believe them, they're trying to hand me anything but the truth, but this case felt different. Darla was odd, and granted I didn't know her well, but the things I did know about her—that she cared deeply for cats; that she was willing to give money, time, and effort to save one sick cat; that though a bit flighty, her heart was in the right place—all led me to believe she was telling the truth.

I got up, retrieved the cups of tea from the kitchen bar, and brought them back to the couch. I handed her hers, then seated myself and took a big sip of mine, no longer piping hot, but revitalizing all the same.

"Let's talk about it. I think we have more information than we know, and together we may come up with an answer."

Darla snuffled, wiped her nose on a linen hankie she produced from a pocket in her red dress, and took a long draught of tea. "I don't know what you're talking about, Lynley, but it sounds serious, and unless you're crazy—which I don't think you are—I'm in."

I laughed. I'd been wondering the same thing about her.

Chapter 21

Cat allergy is one of the most common allergic respiratory diseases, but scientists are working hard on new strategies. Immunotherapy, blocking the immune reaction, and even treating the cats themselves are among promising new methods for combating this disease.

Darla and I talked for a good hour. I began with a rundown on the I-5 Kidnapper since Darla turned out to be one of those fantastical people who avoided the news. I filled her in on the whole thing, from the first disappearance of a young man near Seattle to the recent death of Gerald Sullivan at the busy Hawthorne intersection. As she listened, her face grew ever more horrified, as if she couldn't believe things like that could happen. The possibility seemed to hurt her on a deeply personal level, and I felt bad for being the messenger, but it had to be done if we were going to get to the bottom of things.

After I'd brought Darla up to date with internet articles on my phone, I began to check for something else.

"I-5 *kidnap victims, cats...*" I read as I punched in the words. It was a longshot, but if there was a correlation between the missing men and cats, the web was the place to find it.

A list of links came up, but the headlines featured one subject or the other—not both. Then as I continued to scroll, I came upon a human interest piece written for the

Portland Mercury, a small edition known for giving the weirder side of the news. With a shiver of excitement, I brought up the page, *The I-5 Lost Boys: What Do Cats Have To Do with It?*

Skimming past the sensationalist preliminary paragraphs, I found what I was looking for. The journalist had discovered a strange fact about the four missing men—they all had cats, and those cats were missing as well. There was only one picture, a gorgeous longhair with big round eyes. A bar across the bottom read, "Have you seen me?"

I felt a burst of adrenaline. *Why, yes, dear writer,* I answered in my head, *as a matter of fact, I have.*

I passed the phone to Darla. "Isn't that Newberry?"

She scrutinized the tiny photo, then enlarged it and gasped. "It is! I'm sure of it. That mark over her eyebrow—it's unmistakable." She handed the phone back to me. "But what does this mean?"

"It means I'm right. Somehow the cats you've been receiving from the Stonehenge shelter belong to the kidnap victims. Either your friend Prin or someone else at that shelter knows what's going on."

I finished what was left of my cold tea. "Now it's your turn. Tell me everything you know about Prin, the shelter, and the cats they've been asking you to take."

Darla rose, displacing Oscar who had been her steadfast companion. "Where do I start?"

I thought about it. "Start with the first time you connected with Stonehenge."

Darla paced, skirting the table, the couch, the bookshelf, finally stopping in front of the big bay window where she stared outside with total concentration. Whether she was contemplating the fairy lights and the family of garden gnomes or something within herself wasn't for me to know.

"Like I said, I met Prin online. She was giving a Zoom presentation on caring for cats." She turned to me. "I'm still learning, you see. I never had a cat before a few years ago, never thought I could. I'm deathly allergic. But then my doctor put me on a drug trial for a new allergy medication, specifically designed for cat dander. It worked! Finally I could fulfill my lifelong dream of becoming a cat lady."

That answered one question—why someone with ten cats was such a novice at caring for them—but not the one I needed to know.

"There was something about her," Darla mused. "She seemed so strong, so sure of herself, yet kind at the same time. She fielded all my silly questions and suggested we talk again after the meeting. I leapt at the chance—a one-on-one with this cat expert was something I couldn't turn down. And it wasn't just that—I felt like she really cared."

Cared, or was grooming you for her purpose? I wondered. Already I was thinking of this Prin as the bad guy.

"Go on," I urged, reminding myself I needed to reserve judgment until I'd heard the whole story. For all I knew, Prin was just another pawn in someone else's malevolent plan.

"We got together via Zoom a few times, then she asked if I'd like to meet in person. I agreed instantly. She said to come to the shelter in Marysville, that she had something to show me, something really important. When I got there, she introduced me to Billy."

Gathering the cat in question from his basket by the window, she returned to the couch where she snuggled him in her arms. A roaring purr was the result of her affections.

"Prin said poor Billy had been part of a horrible hoarding situation. She described it in detail, and I was appalled. How people could do such things..." She sighed, curling herself even closer around the cat, as if shielding him from an unseen harm. "Then she told me the shelter had a limit on how many cats they could take at one time, and Billy was over that number. She said she knew he and I would get along and begged me please to adopt him or else he would be euthanized. Don't you see? I had no choice."

I eyed Billy, who showed none of the usual signs of coming from a hoarder. "When was this?"

"Two months ago, in the late summer."

Billy curled out of her grasp and stalked over to me where he settled into my lap. I took the opportunity to give him a quick, unobtrusive checkup. He was smallish for a male but substantial. His full body and glossy coat proved he'd been well-fed and cared for longer than the mere two months with Darla. If this cat lived with hoarders, they weren't like any I'd ever come across.

"Then about three weeks later," Darla continued, "Prin called again. That time it was for Hans."

"What was Han's story?"

"Pretty much the same—Prin said they'd got a big intake and he was the odd cat out."

"Didn't you wonder why the shelter would euthanize a perfectly healthy cat? Most shelters try to place them elsewhere. Northwest Humane takes lots of cats and dogs from smaller shelters when they become overcrowded."

"Really? I didn't know."

"And why was Prin singling you out? She must have known you had a full house already."

"But that's why she chose me. She said since I had so many already, what's one more?"

I shook my head. "That makes no sense whatsoever. Darla, I think you've been duped."

Darla hugged her knees like a little girl. "I did wonder," she said in a whisper. Then her voice grew bolder. "In fact, when I went to get Kitten—Tarzan, you called him?—I asked Prin if I could speak to her supervisor. I wanted to tell him what I thought about his cruel limit policy—give him what's for. I was really angry, as you can imagine. But Prin wouldn't have it. She got weepy and told me if they knew what she'd been doing, she would be fired."

"She was manipulating you," I huffed.

"Or maybe everything she told me was true," Darla countered defensively. "Oh Lynley, this is awful. I don't know what to believe. Is Prin my friend who trusted me with those vulnerable kitty souls or…"

"…is she a kidnapper of men who wants to pawn off their cats where no one will think to look for them?" I finished for her.

Darla shook her head. "How do we find out?"

"There's only one way," I replied resolutely. "Let's pay your Prin a visit."

* * *

It was a bold plan—to seek out a potential kidnapper in her lair—but one that would have to wait. Since it was already well into nighttime when Darla and I finished up our conversation, the only thing we could do was to hold off until morning. The forced delay was both good and bad—it gave me time to mull over what Darla had told me, but it also provided several hours to worry and fret. What would we find when we got to Marysville? Was Prin an evil abductor or a caring shelter employee? It had been simple to convince Darla to go on this fact-finding adventure, but Darla was easily influenced, as proven by her readiness to accept Prin's iffy stories. Would she still want to carry out our plan in the morning, or would she have gone back to thinking of Prin as her best friend? If that were the case, I didn't know what I would do.

I should probably have called the police, but I was still unsure. My instincts told me Prin was neck-deep in whatever was happening with the I-5 Lost Boys, but I could be wrong—she might be just what she put forth to Darla, a caring person who didn't want to see cats needlessly die. If the police went in guns blazing, it could ruin her career, as well as be the end of her friendship with Darla. No, until I had more information, I'd keep it to myself.

I'd volunteered to take Tarzan back to my house, and Darla hadn't objected. Once home, I set him up in the room I keep for my foster cats so he wouldn't be bothered by my curious clowder. He seemed happy to settle into the big kennel with its comfy bed and window looking out over the garden. He ate a bowl of wet food, and by the time I came back with his snack, he was curled up on the plush fast asleep.

I watched him for a few moments, asking myself if I was certain this was indeed Tarzan. I'd only seen Fredric's new companion a few times, and cats can look similar— could I be wrong? If that were the case, it would change everything. But no, I was sure—the distinctive *mip* of a meow and the shoulder jump that Fredric had taught him, to say nothing of his tiny recent neuter scar, proved it beyond a doubt.

"Tarzan," I said softly.

He lifted one eyelid. "*Mip*," he mouthed. Then the eye closed, and he went back to dreaming his kitten dreams.

Chapter 22

Support your local animal shelter. Smaller shelters especially need help in the form of funding and volunteer work. In order to adopt out your furry friends, shelters must have adoption counselors, intake workers, veterinary services, animal socializers, not to mention cleaners who muck out kennels and keep the place sanitary and inviting.

I'd been worried that Darla might have an overnight change of heart, but when we met up the next morning, she was more determined than ever to find out the truth about her so-called friend and the cats she'd been given to "rescue". I'd seen the young cat lady's naïve side, but now she displayed a whole new character—one of a strong woman, willing to accept that she'd been wrong and learn from it. She'd even dressed the part in a gray pantsuit, a black cat print scarf, and a minimum of discrete jewelry. Only her red-orange hair marked her as someone who didn't always comply with the norm.

    It was the first of November, and the weather lived up to that pre-winter gloom in every way. Though it wasn't raining, slate colored clouds hung so low in the overcast sky as to feel ominous. Or maybe that oppressiveness was my imagination—I was wary and anxious and curious like a cat. Were we about to confront a kidnapper, or were we on the wildest of goose chases? I consoled myself with the fact that, either way, I'd get to see the Stonehenge Cat Rescue, a place I'd been meaning to visit for a long time.

We set out for Marysville just before noon. Darla drove her little hybrid car, which gave me time to think. As we wound through the crowded Portland streets and across the Interstate Bridge to the highway, Darla and I chatted, but once we were out of the urban area, the conversation waned. She kept her eyes on the road, and I took in the scenery.

The views were magnificent as we headed east along the Columbia River, the state border between Oregon and Washington. In spite of the gray day, the vast waterway sparkled with an energy of its own. Over on the Oregon side, great boulders rose majestically from the water's edge. Douglas firs stood before them like sentries, green-black against the granite's rain-stained gray. Deciduous trees, bare of foliage, stood out like bald patches within the lush tapestry. No houses or buildings marred the protected landscape.

On our side of the great river, the terrain shifted between flatlands and hills, different but no less picturesque. Every so often, we would pass through a small town with a gas station or a mom-and-pop café. Once, a dog ran into the road, and we both cried out as Darla swerved to miss it.

"That was close," I commented.

"Silly dog," she returned before we lapsed back into silence.

At first the quiet was comfortable, but after a while it became strained. Both Darla and I had questions, and now those questions were becoming, if not elephants in the room, then velociraptors in the vehicle, cougars in the car.

"What do you think…" Darla and I both blurted at the same time.

"You first," Darla laughed.

"No, that's okay," I countered. "You go."

She pursed her lips. "I was just wondering—what are we going to do when we get to the Stonehenge shelter? Do we confront Prin with our suspicions? Or do we play along and see if we can get her to talk about the cats and the men who might really own them?"

"I've been pondering the same thing. I keep going back and forth on how to handle it. I guess all we can do is wait till we get there, then see what happens."

"What if she gets violent? If she did what you said—kidnap and abuse those men—who knows what she's capable of?"

"She's not going to do anything weird at the shelter. You said she's a respected employee there."

"Well, yes, that was my impression, but now that I think back, I'm not so sure. How much of it was a front, with me seeing what I wanted to see?"

"What do you mean?"

Darla's eyes squinted at the road. "It was strange. She always met me in the side parking lot with the cat already packed up in its crate. The only time we went into the building was when we first met up. She gave me a quick tour. She seemed to know the other employees, chatted with them as we went around, but she was doing most of the talking. She was so gregarious—people smiled and responded, but no one actually conversed back and forth like you would imagine. I figured it was because they were busy, but what if they were just being polite?"

"Are you saying she might not be what she led you to believe?"

Darla shrugged. "Maybe she's not an employee at all."

"Then what is she?"

Darla shook her head, at her wit's end. I placed a hand

on her shoulder, careful not to startle her since she seemed tense as a cornered cat.

"Let's try not to overthink it now. Things will come clear soon enough."

Darla seemed to consider what I'd said, then she sighed, "I did it for the cats."

As we entered the little village of Marysville—not much more than a residential district of older homes, a bank, and a few small stores—we again fell silent. Darla made a turn at the stop sign, then another a few blocks down. Finally she pulled up in front of a brick building with big windows and a painted billboard out front, *Stonehenge Cat Rescue*. Below the text was a stylized painting of a cat. The place looked friendly and welcoming, just as a cat shelter should.

She turned off the car, and we stared at each other.

"We're here," she stated needlessly. "Now what?"

A tingle of excitement flashed up my spine, or was it a chill of fear? "Let's go in and ask at the front desk. Maybe we'll learn something there."

Darla gave a solemn nod, and we got out of the car. At the door, we glanced at each other once more, then pushed inside.

Entering the bright, clean lobby, I felt right at home. Happy staff and volunteers were going about with smiles on their faces. Visitors checked out the cats or stood in line at the desk. A few held new adoptions in cardboard carriers. Every so often, there would be a *meow*, *mew*, or *row*, but no sounds of panic or frustration, directly pointing to the good care the felines had been given during their shelter stay.

Down one side of the long room ran a catio housing several cats, all of whom were asleep in their comfy beds.

Opposite was a smaller wire kennel a-wriggle with kittens. Paintings on the walls showed off more of the stylized work by the same artist who had done the sign out front. The bold, colorful lines and rounded figures perfectly illustrated the many spirits of a cat.

I was fascinated by the place, at ease in the shelter surroundings, but Darla hung behind me as if trying to hide in my shadow.

"It's alright," I encouraged her. "Nothing bad is going to happen here, I promise."

She tried to smile, but now I saw yet another side of the woman—Darla was shy. I wouldn't have guessed it from her penchant for outlandish clothing, but I knew sometimes the tendency to outrageousness masks a timid personality.

"Do you see her?" I asked in a low tone. "Prin?"

Darla glanced around the busy room, the staff in their purple scrubs, the yellow-aproned volunteers. "No, she's not here. Oh, well, maybe we should go."

"She might be in the back or on break. I'm going to ask."

I took a deep breath, straightened my shoulders, and walked up to the desk. A middle-aged man greeted me with a crooked but friendly smile.

"Can I help you?"

"I hope so. I'm looking for Prin. Is she on duty today?"

The smile faded, replaced with a questioning look. "Prin Ryder? Hold on, let me ask."

He turned to a woman in a casual floral-patterned suit. "Is Prin here today? This lady wants to know."

The woman's uncertain stare mirrored the man's. "I'm afraid she's not."

I waited for her to elaborate, but she didn't.

"When will she be in?" I pursued when the silence began to stretch.

Again the pair behind the desk exchanged meaningful glances, then the woman, a wide, boxy-framed lady of undetermined but older age, came around to the front and guided me to a vacant bench stacked with cat print pillows.

"Would you and your friend like to have a seat?" The words were kind, but the voice held a frostiness that didn't bode well for what was to come.

Still, what could I say? I sat. Darla took a bit longer to come to terms with the woman's offer, but finally she took a seat beside me. Like two wayward schoolgirls, we stared up at the formidable woman with the distinctively worried look on her mannish face.

"I'm Ava Green, director of Stonehenge Cat Rescue. I'm sorry to have to inform you that Prin Ryder is no longer at this facility."

Another hesitation.

"We had to let her go. We had no choice."

"When did this…?" I began but was interrupted by Darla, who had jumped to her feet.

"Why?" she cried. "What happened? What did she do?"

"I'm afraid I can't divulge that information. It's against our confidentiality policy."

"But I need…" She grabbed Ava Green's sleeve and began to whimper.

Quickly I intervened, unclasping the wayward hand and patting it gently. "It's alright, Darla. Why don't you go wait in the car while I talk to Ms. Green?"

Darla gave me an uncomprehending look. "But what does this mean, Lynley?"

"It's fine. I'll be right out. Okay?"

This time, I gave her a gentle nudge toward the door and a stern stare to make sure she understood. I worried she would balk, but she complied. As she left, she shot me a wistful look. I nodded, then turned back to the flustered director.

"I'm sorry about that. She's new." *New at what?* I was winging it from there on in.

"I'm Lynley Cannon. I'm with Friends of Felines cat shelter in Portland." I reached into my purse and pulled out my badge which I always carried with me in case I had a wild urge to make an impromptu visit to the shelter. I flashed it, hoping she didn't pick up on the place where it read, *Volunteer.* "FOF is urgently looking for Ms. Ryder in relation to some cats she brought us. We need more information on where those cats came from, their previous owners and such."

"You too?" Ava Green retorted. "That's what was happening here as well."

The director glanced over her shoulder, then took a step closer. "I guess I can tell you, since you're from FOF. Prin kept showing up with stray cats that turned out not to be strays. We think she was picking them up from the neighborhoods. I know that in the city people are encouraged to keep their cats indoor-only, but here, many cat owners still allow their cats outside. They are being cared for, mind you. They have good homes, but Prin didn't see it that way. Her heart was in the right place I suppose, trying to make sure those cats were safe, but basically what she did was stealing. We just couldn't have a volunteer taking people's pets, no matter how well-intentioned her motivations."

"So Prin was a volunteer? She gave us the impression

she worked here."

"Oh no, never. She would never have passed our psych evaluation. Among other things, we check for tendencies to hoard. People who work closely with animals may take it a step too far, which can be terrible for both them and the pets. But you know that as a shelter employee yourself."

I did know that. Good will can turn bad if not tempered with restraint and training.

"Thank you for confiding in me," I said somberly, trying to figure out what to do next. "But this news makes it more important than ever that we locate Prin. Could you give me her address?"

"Oh, I'm afraid not," Ava Green burst out. "That would really be going against our rules."

"Please." I smiled, trying not to look like someone who was about to lie through their teeth. "There is more to this investigation than the alleged cat thefts, but I cannot discuss it. We're working with a Northwest Humane Investigator. You can contact Special Agent Denny Paris to confirm," I added.

Denny was both a colleague and a friend, but would he back me up in a fib? I had to hope it wouldn't come to that.

Ava Green's face scrunched up as she considered what I'd said. "Alright, but don't let this come back and bite us. There are channels we should be going through for these sorts of things so we don't get sued."

"I won't disclose the source of the information, I promise."

Again she hesitated, then she straightened her lapel. "Stay here. Ms. Cannon. I'll be right back."

Reseating myself on the bench, I turned to look at the cats in the catio. A tabby with amber eyes was staring straight at me. I gave her a slow blink, and she blinked back. I was pleased to hear her start up a roaring purr.

"What's going on?" Darla whispered as she slipped in beside me.

I glared at her. "I've got it covered. Please, just be quiet and control yourself."

"I'm sorry. I get emotional. But I'll be good."

Ava Green returned with a slip of paper. She looked questioningly at Darla, but true to her word, the young cat lady just gave a polite smile and kept her mouth shut.

Ava furtively passed me the note. "Here you go."

I opened it to read in crisp cursive, *The Alhambra Motel, 14 River Road, Marysville.*

"She lives in a motel?"

Ava nodded. "Yes, but she's the only one there. The place has been shut down for years. I think she made some arrangement with the owners. Now, remember what you promised," she added with a scowl.

I gave her a sly smile. "We were never here."

Chapter 23

Though the average lifespan of a cat is between thirteen and seventeen years, cats are living into their twenties with the advancement of good care. The longest-lived cats on record survived into their thirties.

According to the GPS in Darla's car, the Alhambra Motel wasn't far, only a little way out of Marysville and up in the hills. The hybrid took the winding roads easily, and before I knew it, we were well into the wilds.

"Why would someone build a motel all the way out here?" Darla posed.

"Marysville used to be a big port for ships coming up the Columbia, but then the river was dredged so they could make it into Portland. According to Wikipedia," I added. "There must have been all sorts of dock worker's accommodations back then."

But now those amenities were long gone. My question, more to the point than the location of the motel, was why Prin would choose to live there in the first place.

I peered out at the thick forest, the lofty trees, the clumps of rain-slick sword fern and salal that dotted the forest floor. Beyond the first few feet lit by the car's headlamps, the scene diminished into shadow. I glanced at the clock—a little before five. The daytime was dwindling, and the dense woods were dark as full night.

To add to the gloom, it had begun to rain again. Darla started her wipers, first intermittently, then full on. The rhythmic clack, clack, clack, was nerve wracking, like claws on a chalkboard as I sat rigid in my seat. The conversation with Ava Green had been enlightening, but not in a good way. The more I learned about Prin Ryder, the more curious I became, and the more afraid.

I'd filled Darla in on everything Ava had told me—Prin's strange penchant for picking up other people's cats and her subsequent dismissal from Stonehenge—so when Darla said out of the blue, "This is getting creepy," I knew exactly what she meant.

"Seeking out Prin in her home lair?" she continued. "Don't you think that's creepy, Lynley?"

"We don't have to do this," I replied. "Going to Prin's house was never part of the plan."

"It could be dangerous. Prin must have really messed up to be let go from the shelter—they don't usually fire volunteers, do they?"

"According to Ava Green, she'd been acting strangely from the very start. When Prin met you last night to give you Tarzan, she'd already been dismissed."

Darla adjusted her rearview mirror, as if she expected someone to be following her—or maybe she wished they were, so we didn't seem quite so alone. "I say we turn around and go back to town, get hold of the police and…"

"…tell them what we know?" I finished for her. "Let the professionals follow up if they think it's something?" But then I gave a huff. "Though a batch of poached cats doesn't seem like much of a lead."

"If she was doing it all along—swiping neighborhood cats and bringing them to the shelter—Newberry, Hans, and the others she gave me might have nothing to do with…"

"…the Lost Boys?" I filled in once more. "I get what

you're saying. But we saw that photo of Newberry in the Mercury article. And what about Tarzan? He is without a doubt my neighbor's kitten. Unless I'm way off base, Prin couldn't have picked him up here in Marysville."

"So it's agreed we go home," Darla bluntly put forth. "Someone else can unravel this mystery. I need to give Sheba her meds."

It was the safest—the *only* thing to do. With a sigh, I replied reluctantly, "It's agreed."

I felt immediately relieved, but my relief was edged with guilt. If Prin was the kidnapper, she could be holding those men somewhere nearby. Who knew what horrors they were going through at that very moment? Could we do something to save them? Not if we turned away.

Darla had no such qualms. She was already slowing the car to find a turnaround.

Peering through the slants of rain, she said, "There's a pullout just ahead. I'm going for it, okay?"

"Okay," I replied dully, the welfare of those victims weighing on my heart like a four hundred-pound lion.

The car slid into the muddy pullout, but as Darla headed into a U-turn, her headlights caught a darkened lane off to the right. Beside the entrance hung a dilapidated sign—*The Alhambra*.

She jerked the vehicle to a stop, and we both bent forward to stare. Red block letters, hand-painted on a black background, the placard was chipped but readable. Dangling beneath it on one link was a smaller board, *No Vacancy*.

"It's a sign," Darla whispered.

"Yes, it is," I replied, studying the wooden square.

"No, I mean the other kind of sign, a portent. We have to go on now."

I wasn't surprised that the young woman believed in portents. I did too, for that matter, though I wasn't convinced this was one of them. Still, there we were, the place we'd been searching for. If not a sign, it was at the very least synchronic.

I peered down the shadowed drive. "We still don't have to go in. Dangerous, remember? Let the pros handle it, we decided—right?"

But it was too late—Darla was already pulling the car around and heading into the tiny road.

"Okay, I guess we're doing this," I mumbled, grabbing hold of the hand bar to soften the bumps of the rutted way.

Once we were through a perimeter of trees, the scene abruptly changed. At one time, there had been gardens and a massive lawn, but neglect had diminished them to a mess of tangled weeds. Vines and brambles encroached onto the road, as if it were rarely used. There were no lights to break the slick black night, and I wondered if we'd got it wrong—that instead of Prin and her kidnap victims, the only things we would find in this lonely place would be ghosts of abandonment.

We passed another sign. *Visit the Alhambra* could just be made out beneath a modern placard of the sort one can buy at a hardware store—*No Trespassing - Keep Out!* Darla saw it too, but neither of us commented. Neither of us said a word.

A little farther on, the driveway made a sharp turn and there it was, the Alhambra in all its decaying glory. Darla pulled to a stop and gaped at the structure that now loomed before us.

The place was not large, only two stories with a peaked roof, but it had been designed to look like a mini mansion. Painted wooden pillars, now chipped and peeling, did their best to hold up the covered front porch. The broad stairway sagged to one side. On a hulking red door had been painted the word *Office*, but so long ago it now appeared more like arcane symbols than letters. There was a light inside. Through a set of dirty windows, I could see the silhouette of a cat.

"This must be it," I said needlessly.

Darla hadn't moved since she'd turned off the car. Now she rolled down the window. Outside was perfectly silent—not a sound coming from the dark woods. Straining our ears as one does when accustomed to being surrounded with noise, we listened to the nothing.

"What should we…" I was starting to say when I heard it—a soft, muffled cry. Cat? Coyote? *Human*?

As quickly as it started, it was gone, but its echo still rang in my mind, not from the house but somewhere off to the side. In the gleam of the headlights, I could just make out a second building, a long, low structure, reminiscent of budget motels built in the sixties. At least that was my impression—beyond a single curtained window and a once-turquoise door with a numeral *One* painted on it, the scene faded into the night like a horror movie.

"Now what?" I whispered.

Darla just looked at me, eyes wide and probing.

Then her gaze slipped past me. A forceful rap sounded on the window, making me jump. I whipped around to see someone staring in. The face was in shadow, but the silhouette against the light from the office door which now stood open, seemed huge.

The face lingered a moment, then disappeared around the back of the car and came up on Darla's side.

"Dee!" she roared through the window. "What the dragon's teeth are you doing here?"

Chapter 24

Cats (and other companion animals) have a way of touching their person's heart like no human can.

Prin, for I knew it must be she, flung the door open and pulled Darla outside. Instantly someone else took her place in the driver's seat—a large and ancient long-furred Persian of a light butter color. He looked me in the eyes and gave a little *prrup*.

"Maz, get out of there," Prin commanded, but her tone was gentle. When the cat held his own, she reached in and picked him up. Then, with Maz cradled in her arms, she turned back to Darla who was cringing against the car as if she'd been hit.

"What's up, Dee?" Prin asked. Her voice was deep and welcoming. "Is something wrong with the cats?"

"No... Not the cats but..."

"But what, Dee?" Now the voice held a hint of darkness. "Go on. Tell me."

"I... I..." Darla stuttered. "I mean, we..."

I got out of the car and came around to her side. I didn't want Darla blurting the whole tale before we knew what we were up against. If Prin was innocent of the kidnappings, it would sound crazy and insulting. If she was guilty, a couple of cat ladies confronting her with her crime could be, well, as we'd speculated previously, dangerous.

"Hello," I stepped forward, insinuating myself

between Prin and Darla. "I'm Lynley. Pleased to meet you," I added, holding out a hand.

Prin looked at it. A flicker of emotion crossed her face, but I couldn't tell what it meant, so quickly was it replaced by a thin smile.

"Prin Ryder," she replied, taking the hand lightly.

Now that the glow from the office door was no longer behind her, I could see she was, though a hefty girl, not nearly as big as I'd first imagined. Her choice of clothing, loose jeans and a plaid wool hunter's jacket, gave the impression of bulk. Her long, straight hair was done up in a sloppy knot on top of her head. I still couldn't tell the color of her eyes, but they were large and questioning, like those of a vintage doll.

"I'm from Friends of Felines cat shelter," I said for no good reason. "Darla told me you'd helped her adopt some cats."

"That's right. What about it?"

Okay, what about it? I asked myself.

"I'm concerned. Darla already has a full house," I stated honestly, "but you keep giving her more, and it seems she can't say no to a cat in need." I paused, wondering where to go from there. Then I had an idea. I'd be winging it, soaring into fantasyland, but if it got me the information I needed, I didn't mind telling a few lies.

"We were wondering," I began slowly, letting the concept form in my head, "if there was a way to return one or two to their original owners. Possibly the most recent one, the tabby kitten you gave her last night."

"Oh, really?" Prin turned to Darla. "Why, Dee, you never told me you were full up."

Darla stared at the ground. "I didn't want to say anything, but I do have quite a few cats now, what with the others from Stonehenge and my original crew." Her pleading eyes rose to meet Prin's. "You told me if I didn't take them they would be euthanized. I couldn't stand that."

"No one wants that," I broke in. "But couldn't you at least see if the kitten's original person would take him back? If money was the issue, I'm sure Friends of Felines could help with expenses. We have a fund for that."

"He's dead," Prin spat. "The relatives didn't want the cat and brought him to Stonehenge to be put to sleep."

Now it was Prin who was doing the winging because I knew for a fact she was lying like a rug.

"But couldn't he have been adopted out through your shelter? He's a kitten, after all. Everybody wants kittens."

"Nobody wanted that one, believe me," she huffed. "I wouldn't have bothered Dee if there had been any other way."

I shoved the first part of her crazy statement—that no one would want a gorgeous, healthy, recently neutered kitten like Tarzan—to the back of my mind and moved on to the second.

"I'm sorry, but I find it strange that you're handing off all these cats to Darla instead of adopting them out through the system. I know how shelters work, and that's not the way."

Prin's fake smile vanished, and for a moment, she openly glared. Then her face reset into a façade of innocence, and she turned to Darla.

"But Dee, you told me you wanted the cats. Don't you remember? You wanted to rescue them and give them a good home." Her voice was low, almost hypnotic, and suddenly I saw how she manipulated the shy Darla.

Darla looked more uncomfortable than ever. "Yes,

well, I may have said something like that. But last night I did mention the kitten had to be the last one."

Prin gazed thoughtfully into the darkness and gave a great sigh. "Yes, of course. And I totally understand. From now on, I'll just leave those poor unadoptable cats to their fate. If they are put down, well…"

"No!" Darla cried. "Not that! Anything but that!"

I had to do something before Darla began making promises she couldn't keep.

"I don't understand," I intervened. "What makes those particular cats unadoptable?" I shook my head. "You must have some strange restrictions at Stonehenge. Tar… I mean, the kitten seemed perfectly adoptable to me."

Rats! I'd slipped up. Had she caught me? I couldn't be sure.

"Stonehenge is a small shelter," Prin said evasively. "There are many reasons why we can't take a cat. We try to hand them off to other shelters, but sometimes too many come at once. Darla isn't the only person to help out. I take some of them myself."

She sounded so sincere, so matter of fact, and what she said made sense—smaller shelters didn't have nearly the resources of ones like Friends of Felines and Northwest Humane. Except I knew she was lying, and that made her whole speech moot.

Her voice bit into my reflection. "Here, let me show you."

Without waiting for a reply, she put her cat down on the ground and began toward the motel building. The cat followed, tail high in the air like a fluffy banner.

Darla started after them, but I grabbed her arm. "You really want to go off into the dark with that woman?"

"Uh, I don't know… She did ask nicely."

"That doesn't mean she's nice," I hissed back.

Prin turned, and though I knew she couldn't have overheard me, I felt guilty. "Well, come on. You want to see my fosters, don't you?"

I recalled the cry I'd heard earlier. Could she be telling the truth, at least about the cats?

But Tarzan... my brain reminded me yet again.

"Maybe another time," I replied ambiguously. "Darla and I really need to get going. We have to be back in town."

Prin swung around to face us, still edging toward the motel but now walking backwards. "Are you sure? It won't take but a moment. I've got three tabbies and a Maine Coon mix. They're oh so sweet!" She gave a persuasive smile. "Who knows, Lynley? Maybe you'll want to adopt one yourself."

She took a few more backward steps. It was a strange thing to do, and it threw me off my guard.

"Come on," Prin teased. "Come see the cats. You know you want to."

Now that my eyes had adjusted to the dark, I could make out the one-story building more clearly, six units with turquoise trim and doors all in a row. A cracked concrete walk ran along the front, weeds sprouting through the fractures. The place seemed about as inviting as a prison.

So far Darla was standing her ground, but I didn't know how much longer that would last. It was obvious Prin still had a hold over her, and her instinct was to obey. Since I couldn't physically force Darla back into the car, I'd have to stop it another way, but Prin was a good talker. Heck, I wanted to see those cats in Number One as much as Darla did. A big Maine Coon? Who could resist? And I had a soft spot for tabbies—the bright red boys like my own Big Red as well as the black, brown, and silvers like Tarzan.

Tarzan! The thought of the kitten snapped me back to reality. This was no time to go cat-seeing—I needed to save Tarzan's dad.

Prin was nearly to the door of the first unit, still walking backwards with her arms extended in a gracious gesture, when her heel caught the edge of the walkway. She let out a sharp scream as she buckled and fell, her head hitting the cement with a thunk so loud it sent Maz running. For a moment, she lay motionless, half on the grass and half on the stoop. Then she turned her head, her big eyes upon us. In a low moan, she uttered a single, forced word: "Help..."

Darla was already running to her side. There was no stopping her now, nor did there seem to be a reason. Prin was, at best, incapacitated, if not badly hurt.

Darla fell to a crouch at the woman's side. "Prin! Are you okay?"

Prin blinked up at her. "No, I don't think so." She tentatively touched her scalp where she'd hit it, then drew her hand back and looked. No blood, thank goodness. "I feel dizzy. Help me sit up."

Darla put an arm around her and began to ease her into a sitting position, but Prin cried out. "Oh, it hurts. My ankle—I think it's sprained. That was really stupid of me, falling like that," she added weakly. "I was just so excited for you to see my fosters."

"I'd better call 911." I started to the car for my phone.

"Lynley, wait!" Prin cried. "Don't do that. Just help me into the unit. There's a bed in there where I can lie down."

"If you have a concussion, you should be seen," I told

her.

"No, please," she snapped back. "I just need to rest a few minutes. I don't want to go to the hospital. I don't have any insurance."

I sympathized. Being uninsured meant that trip would bring thousands of dollars of debt, something no one wanted to incur unless there was no other choice. There would still be time to call the ambulance if we deemed it necessary.

"Come on, Lynley, let's do as she asks," said Darla. "We'll be better able to see how badly she's hurt once we get her into the light."

"Okay, I guess." I advanced toward the injured woman. "You take that side—I'll get the door."

Prin was not a light person, and Darla and I struggled to heft her onto the little stoop. I grabbed the rusty doorknob of Unit One and pushed the old door wide so we could get her inside. It was a clumsy business, and Prin seemed about as cooperative as a dead weight.

We were nearly across the threshold when Prin shouted, "Shut it quick! Don't let the cats out!"

Instinctively I slammed the door behind us, no novice to keeping cats corralled. As it closed, the room was plunged into black.

"Where's the light switch, Prin?" I felt along the wall. "I can't see a thing."

Instead of answering, she shrugged out of my grasp. I felt a vicious thrust as she shoved me across the room. Now it was my turn to trip and fall. My glasses went flying, but I came down on something soft.

I heard a scuffle and a small cry. When the light finally came on, I saw we were in trouble.

I was on a dilapidated bed. Darla was on the floor—

apparently Prin had pushed her too, but she'd landed in a less fortunate location. Prin stood sentry by the door, her face full of rage. All signs of her previous malaise were gone now—a trick, I realized, to get us where she wanted us, and it had worked to perfection.

"You had to go sticking your nose in my business," Prin accused. "Darla, I thought we had a rapport. After all, you're a cat person..." She turned her hateful gaze on me. "And you, Lynley Cannon, you said you were too. I should never have listened to either of you."

She shuffled on her feet, turning her eyes to the cracked ceiling.

"All I want to do is save cats," she stammered. "And now look what you've done. You've ruined everything!"

In a swift move that proved beyond all doubt her injuries had been faked, she opened the door, spun outside, then slammed it so hard the room shook. As I leapt after her, I heard the lock set. I was too late.

Still, I grabbed the knob, turning it without success, then rattling it with all the rage and frustration built up in me. I'd ignored my own warnings and let Prin win.

Chapter 25

Cats are creatures of habit. When their routine is upset or their dinner runs late, chances are you will hear about it.

Darla pulled herself from the dusty floor into a tattered armchair. "It's not the poor door's fault we let the bad lady trap us in here."

The comment was almost humorous, and I would have laughed under less desperate circumstances.

With one last impotent shake, I let go of the knob and turned away. "You're right. It's not the door's fault—it's mine."

"No, Lynley, it's mine," Darla mumbled. "I should have known something was up with Prin. You know, I believed in her right up until the end? Even after you laid out all the facts, I still didn't think she was guilty. I didn't want her to be guilty." She shook her head as a tear coursed down her cheek. "I didn't want our friendship to be a lie."

I moved to the distraught woman and took her hand. In the unheated room, her fingers were cold as ice.

"Of course you didn't. You're a good person, Darla. You look for the good in others. There's nothing wrong with that."

"Except when that person happens to be a crazed criminal."

I shrugged. "We don't expect people to be liars. We take them at face value and hope for the best. Sometimes we get burnt."

"In this case, I think *roasted* is a better word."

She fell silent as we both tried to grasp what had occurred. Darla may have led a relatively crime-free life, but I'd been in bad situations before. I wasn't sure I could take another one. Whoever said what doesn't kill you makes you stronger should be ashamed of himself. I certainly didn't feel stronger for everything I'd been through. Quite the opposite—I feared another brush with danger might put me right over the edge.

"What should we do?"

"Huh?" I shook off my morose reflections and looked at Darla. She remained pensive, but she'd wiped away the tear. Now, with her face set in determination, I doubted there would be another.

"What do we do now?" she repeated. "How do we get ourselves out of this mess?"

As if in response to her own question, she rose to her feet and started moving around the unit, making a thorough inspection as she went. One room and a bathroom, there was little to see, but she proceeded to go over every inch.

She began with the door, which as I'd already determined, was locked. She bent to peer at the locking mechanism, then uttered a harrumph and moved on to the window. She pulled the shoddy curtain aside and stared out into the night. From where I stood by the chair, I could only see blackness and the stark reflection of the room.

"Anything?" I asked through my anxiety.

She ran her fingers along the sill, then up the chipped moldings and around the old-fashioned eight-inch panes. "Even if we broke the glass, we couldn't get out. The panes are too small."

"But aren't motel units required to have a second exit in case of fire? No, probably not back when this was built," I answered for myself.

Darla stepped over to the bed and felt around the edges of the old mattress, then peered underneath it.

"These yours?" She handed me my glasses.

"Thanks." I straightened the frame and slipped them on. "That's better. Or maybe not," I added. Now that I could see clearly, the place looked bleaker than ever.

Darla bent down to peek under the bed itself. "An impressive collection of dust kittens," she commented, then moved on to the night table. After checking the exterior, both front and back, she carefully pulled out the single drawer. Reaching in, she picked up the old, black-bound bible and held it high.

"Gideon has been here."

"We might need that before this is over," I quipped, though it wasn't really a joke.

Deciding it was time to get off my rear end and join the search, I went to the only other piece of furniture in the room, a credenza with a huge mirror. At first, I thought the mirror was part of the cabinet, but it turned out to be a separate piece propped up behind. It was screwed flat against the wall, so no hidden compartments or secret panels. There was nothing in the drawers, not even dust. That was a dead end as well.

Darla had disappeared into the bathroom, and I heard running water, then the flush of the toilet.

"Good news," she said, coming out again. "The plumbing is functional. At least we won't have to die with full bladders."

"You seem awfully flippant for someone imprisoned by a maniac," I charged.

"Denial," she answered matter-of-factly.

Going back to her chair, she plopped down and drew up her knees. "Let's brainstorm."

I crumpled onto the bed feeling utterly defeated. Usually I'm the one who comes up with the ideas, who supports others, who finds the silver lining in the blackest of clouds, but not this time. This time it would have to be my strange young crazy cat lady client doing the heavy lifting. I just couldn't summon the courage.

But giving up wasn't an option, and I knew that. Bracing myself against the old headboard, I worked to get my thoughts in line.

"I don't think Prin wants to hurt us," Darla mused, oblivious to my turmoil. "But our coming here definitely wasn't part of her agenda." Darla sighed. "Do you still figure she kidnapped those men?"

"You mean maybe she's just a cat lady with a warped sense of right and wrong? But that doesn't explain why she locked us in here," I followed up. "And it doesn't explain Tarzan. He is my neighbor's cat. Fredric went missing a few days ago, and now she turns up with his cat?"

"Are you sure your neighbor's missing and isn't just off doing man things? And I have to ask, are you absolutely certain the kitten I brought home is Tarzan?"

"Yes to both." Then I faltered. "Well, almost certain. I don't know. I don't know anything right now except that we need to get out of this room."

"You're right about that. Got any ideas?"

There was a pause.

"No."

Another pause.

"And you know what else?"

"No, what?"

"Prin said there would be cats in here, tabbies and a Maine Coon." My gaze mournfully panned the room. "She was lying about that too."

* * *

Darla and I had left our phones in the car, thinking we wouldn't be staying at the Alhambra for any length of time. Now I felt naked without that important instrument. Moreso, I felt lost. There would be no phoning for help or even knowing the time of day. I guessed it must have been around six, but there was no way to be sure, and the time warp would get worse the longer we remained trapped.

"Do you think anyone will miss us?" Darla asked wistfully. Her strong start was fading, and without that positive energy, I feared what would happen next.

"My cats will miss me," I said in as firm a tone as I could muster. "It should be around their dinnertime. At least yours have the automatic feeders."

"Yes, but feeders have to be refilled, and Sheba needs her medicine. How long do you guess Prin will keep us here?"

That was one question among many for which I had no answer. I worked to think them through.

First off, what was Prin up to? Was she unbalanced, or was she truly a criminal?

Furthermore, why had she locked us in a room instead of just letting us be on our way? She must have known we suspected something and saw us as a threat. She said we had ruined her plans. What plans?

What did she intend to do with us now that she had us? She wouldn't simply come back and say it was all a mistake and have a nice day. No, the chances of that were slim to none.

That brought me to the final question, which had been the big one all along: How to escape?

I was thinking of taking another tour around the room—look for something we might have missed such as a tool we could use to force the lock or a Twilight Zone portal to another dimension—when I heard a scratching sound coming from behind the credenza. I froze and shot a glance at Darla. Sitting tall with her eyes wide, I knew she'd heard it too.

"Oh, no," she hissed. "Not rats! I really hate rats."

Though I had no real fear of the little mammals, I didn't want them in my house, let alone in the same small room where I'd been caged by a killer. The clawing grew louder—if they were rats, they were big ones.

The mirror behind the credenza began to rattle and shake, as if some great pressure was building on the other side. In an eruption of breaking glass, it burst outward, the frame tearing apart at its corners and sharp shards exploding throughout the room. With a shrill scrape, the little credenza pushed forward to topple and splinter as the cheap piece hit the ground, adding to the maelstrom.

Instinctively I covered my eyes. When I dared to look again, I found myself staring at a hole in the wall. Except it wasn't a hole, it was a door connecting our room with the next. From the darkness, I heard a grunt and a moan. A man moved into the doorway, unkempt and naked from the waist up. He took a tentative step forward before collapsing on top of the fallen credenza with a groan.

Darla grabbed the only defensive weapon in the room, the Gideon bible, and was heading for the newcomer.

"Wait!" I cried. "It's Fredric!"

I hurried to his aid, Darla a step behind me, still

holding the bible.

"Put down that book and help me get him onto the bed," I ordered. "Grab the blanket—he must be freezing! Oh, my goodness," I whispered. "Fredric!"

Fredric was weak but determined. With our assistance, he made it to the bed where he gratefully wrapped the blanket around himself. His eyes focused on me, and he blinked in surprise.

"Lynley?"

"It's me, Fredric. And my friend Darla. Are you okay?" It was a ridiculous question—besides nearly fainting on the threshold, he looked worse than a street cat who'd been left out for too long. His eyes were puffy red, and his lips chapped. His face held a deadly pallor, and even though he'd been gone for a mere few days, he seemed to have lost weight.

"Bring him some water," I charged.

Darla scurried into the bathroom, coming out a moment later with a paper cup.

"Not the cleanest, I don't imagine, but it was all I could find."

The young man took it in both hands, then gulped it greedily as if he hadn't drunk in days—which I realized may have been the truth.

"Better," he sighed. "The sink's turned off in my luxury suite. There's the toilet, but I haven't got that desperate." He nodded toward the unit next door, then looked me in the eye. "Are you an angel?"

He winked, and I knew, if nothing else, Fredric hadn't lost his sense of humor.

"No, not an angel, dear boy. Unfortunately, we're locked in here too."

"Wasn't sure I was going to make it," he sighed. "Then

I heard noises over here. I hadn't heard anything for—" He sat up abruptly. "What day is it? How long have I been here? She's got shutters over the window so I can't tell if it's day or night." His body gave an inadvertent jerk. "We have to get out of here, Lynley. That woman is out of her mind."

"Prin?"

He nodded.

"I thought as much. But we've tried. The door's locked and the window has eight-inch panes. I don't know how to pick the lock, but even if I did, we've got nothing to pick it with. What about your room? Is there something in there that could help?"

"I used a pin I found on the floor to finagle the lock between our rooms," said Fredric, "but it broke in the mechanism. I can try to get it out…" He made to sit but fell back against the pillow.

"That's okay. We'll figure something out. What about you?" I called to Darla who had slipped next door while I was tending to Fredric. "Anything?"

"Nope, not a darned thing." She leaned against the jamb. "But Lynley, you've got to see this."

I stared at her, uncomprehending. She gave a nod and ducked into the adjoining unit.

"I'll be right back," I said to Fredric. "You don't go anywhere, okay?"

He smiled and closed his eyes. "I promise."

I crossed to the newly revealed door. Darla moved aside, her face drawn, and I peered in.

"This is where your friend has been all that time," she intoned.

"Lights?" I asked.

She shook her head. "None. But it gets worse. Come

on, I'll show you."

I stepped across the threshold and immediately felt the temperature plunge.

"The air conditioner is on full blast, and there's no way to turn it off."

"Why on Earth would she...?" But glancing around me, I knew. Prin wanted the place to be as uncomfortable for her victim as possible.

A beam of light from behind me shone on a single metal chair. Underneath the chair I could see something white, remnants of zip ties. Had Fredric been bound? But that made sense. She wouldn't want him to get away. Yet he did get away! *Good for him*, I thought to myself, until I had the revelation that he was still just as trapped as before, but in more comfortable accommodations.

I shuddered. Cold, dark, and trussed up like a holiday turkey. What had poor Fredric done to deserve such treatment?

Darla slipped past me into our unit, and I followed, closing the door tight behind me. I knew without further scrutiny there was nothing in that awful room to help us out of our fix.

Chapter 26

Cats sleep a lot, but even at rest, their hearing and sense of smell remains on alert.

Fredric was up when we returned, and with the blanket wrapped around his shoulders, was exploring the room, much the same as Darla and I had done previously. He seemed better now that he was warm, hydrated, and in the company of others. Hopefully together we could come up with a way to escape.

"So how long have I been here?" he asked again.

"Today is Sunday," I said softly. "It's November first."

He spun around and gave me a panicked look. "I missed the play? Everyone must hate me." I could hear in his head, ...*the show must go on*.

"The play was fine. Your understudy did a good job, and Seleia was brilliant at covering a few slips. It's not as if you skipped it on purpose, Fredric. You weren't given any choice. I'm sure you would much rather have been there than here."

"That's an understatement," he mumbled, but even at that low tone, I could hear the vehemence.

"What happened?" I inquired. "If you feel up to telling us."

Fredric completed his uneventful circuit of the room with no revelations and went back to sit on the bed. His eyes slipped shut and he shook his head.

"Prin," he uttered with such hatred and fear that the

words nearly knocked me back.

"She captured you? But how? Why?"

"I don't know. I'd only met her a few times. She was an extra in the last production I worked on. She seemed nice. I asked her out once, or I should say she asked me. Seleia and I had been fighting—Seleia wanted to see other people. I was mad, so when I ran into Prin at the Coffee Palace and she suggested we have coffee together, I didn't see the harm."

He turned to Darla. "Do you think you could get me a little more water? That was part of Prin's torture. No food or drink. No light. Cold as a..." His eyes were haunted as the sentence hung in the air.

Darla returned with another full cup. He quaffed a big gulp, then forced himself to go at it more slowly.

"But how did you get from coffee to being kidnaped?" I pressed as gently as I could. I knew it was hard for him, but I needed the answer.

"I'd rather forget it, but I know how you are, Lynley. Your curiosity's not going to let it go, is it?"

"There might be some clue," I justified. "Something we can use to help us escape."

He sighed. "Okay, I guess remembering can't make things any worse than they already are."

He took another sip of water and cleared his throat. "Coffee went fine. We talked about nothing in particular. Then I mentioned Tarzan. Once I said I had a kitten at home she was all about going to see him. I didn't want to take her, but she wore me down. It was close by, and I figured what could it hurt? I hadn't brought my car, so she drove me back to my place."

He hesitated, then gave a little snarl. "That's when it went pear-shaped. As soon as we got in the door, she started coming on to me. I wasn't having it and told her flat out I had a girlfriend. At first, she was angry—no one likes being rejected—but then she seemed to settle down. We talked a while longer. She had some questions about the film industry and then we got onto cats. She asked if she could have a drink. I think she meant alcohol, but I offered her tea. She must have slipped something into mine, because the next thing I knew, I woke up in that room next door with a killer headache and no recollection of how I got here."

He swigged a bit more water.

"I had no idea where I was," he continued, his voice growing more subdued. "It was dark—I couldn't see anything. My hands and feet were zip tied to a chair, and it was freezing. Things get a little fuzzy there—I remember yelling until my voice was gone and trying to get loose, but all I managed to do was tip the chair over and get myself stuck in a lousy position on the floor. After what seemed like hours, Prin came in with a flashlight. That was the first I'd seen of my surroundings. I was already scared, but that sight took it to a whole new level."

"We've seen it," I told him. "Pretty grim."

"Really grim. I was sure she was going to kill me then and there—at that point I almost hoped she would and get it over with. Anything would have been better than the suspense of being holed up in that place, not knowing when the axe would fall. But she didn't kill me. She unhooked me from the chair, got me upright, and clipped off the ties around my wrists. She pointed to the bathroom and told me that was where I could do my business. That's when I realized she'd taken my shirt."

"Did she say anything else? Tell you why she was doing this to you?"

"Mostly she was silent, silent like a rock. But at one point she said something like, 'That's what you get for shunning me.'" Then she added, "'That's what you all get.'"

I felt myself shiver at the implications. "All?"

Fredric sighed heavily. "Yeah, Lynley. I didn't know what it meant at the time, but I soon found out. I'm not the only one here. There was a guy in the room next to me, and he said there was someone else next to him."

Fredric's account corresponded with my theory that the motel was where Prin was holding her victims.

"Could you communicate with him?"

"Yes, at first. We had some shouted conversations, but then he stopped answering. I hoped he'd escaped somehow, but I think he just got too weak to yell anymore. And as to the question you're about to ask, Lynley, no, he didn't know any more than I did about what was going on. But he did confirm one thing. He told me his name was Guy, Guy Ward. I recognized it from the news—one of the I-5 Lost Boys. That's when I knew I'd been taken by the kidnapper."

Fredric's voice faded, though he looked as if he wanted to say more. I gave him time.

"But how did you find me?" he finally posed, his turn to query. "*I don't even know where I am.*"

"You're a little way out of Marysville, Washington at the defunct Alhambra Motel."

"What? Really?" I could see the wheels turning. "Wow."

"And as for your other question, how Darla and I ended up here, that's a long story, beginning with your cat."

Fredric sat up abruptly. "Tarzan? Is Tarzan okay? She

didn't take him too and do something terrible?"

"As a matter of fact, she did take him, but she didn't hurt him, and we got him back."

"How?" he stammered.

"Long story, remember? But he's fine and resting comfortably at my house."

I went ahead and summarized everything that had gone down since Darla showed up last night with his kitten in tow. Darla filled in about her relationship with Prin and how the pseudo-shelter employee had tricked her into taking the cats. When we finished, Fredric gave me a look of pure exasperation.

"I thought you'd know better by now than to get yourself mixed up in risky situations…" He grinned and grabbed my hand. "But I'm so glad you did. Now let's get the heck out of here."

"You're right about that. We've got to find a way out, and the sooner the better."

"And we need to save the others," Fredric declared. "From what I read in the news before I…" His voice wavered. "Well, there should be four more."

"There are six units," said Darla. "Not including ours, do you think she's got a victim locked up in each one?"

I thought about Gerald Sullivan but said nothing. He'd escaped, but too late. If only he'd survived long enough to tell his story, we wouldn't have been in this predicament.

"Does Prin ever come to check on you?"

Fredric shook his head. "She hasn't been back since that first time. I imagine leaving us alone is part of the shunning."

"Shunning?" I studied the young man. "You used that word before, or to be accurate, you said Prin used it."

"I guess I did. It's not something I know much about,

but it sure feels awful to have someone treat you like you don't exist."

"The act of shunning is regarded as a form of abuse and torture," I said. "Could that be what she had in mind?"

"Yes, that's exactly what she had in that warped, convoluted, evil mind of hers!"

"Do you suppose she mistook your rejection of her advances for some sort of shun?" asked Darla.

"You might be onto something," I contemplated, then turned to Fredric. "And to get revenge, she drugged you and put you in isolation, or in other words, shunned you back. Darla, you may have just uncovered the motive for the kidnappings."

"It's not such a stretch as you might think," she replied. "Prin told me she'd had an unhappy childhood. She didn't elaborate except to say she'd been shunned by her parents. I thought it a strange turn of phrase at the time, then forgot all about it—until now."

"Well, motive or not," said Fredric, "that doesn't get us any closer to an escape plan. I think we've pretty well established she's not coming back for me, but what about you two? You're a whole different matter. Maybe she'll treat you better."

I turned to Darla. "You've had the most experience with her. Do you think she'll come back tonight?"

"I don't know. She's always been nice to me before."

"Nice?" I huffed, not in the mood for Darla's blind sanguinity. "Like manipulating you into doing her dirty work?"

"Maybe so, but underneath it all," Darla defended sulkily, "she just wanted to save cats."

"Cats she stole when she abducted their cohabitors.

How can you overlook that?"

"I'm not," Darla muttered. I was about to shoot her another caustic remark when she added, "But to answer your question, yes, I think she'll come back."

My criticism wasn't helping matters. Taking a breath, I switched tracks.

"What if Fredric hides in the bathroom while we wait for her? I'm pretty sure the three of us could overpower her if we caught her by surprise."

Fredric cringed. "Back into the dark? Just to sit there waiting?"

I touched his arm. "I know it's scary, but you can have the light on. Please, Fredric. It's going to take all three of us to bring her down—she's a beefy girl."

"In case you haven't noticed..." He gave an apologetic smile. "I'm not at my best."

"She may not come for hours," said Darla. "I don't know about you two but I'm no good at waiting."

"Yeah, that idea doesn't sound as great as it did in my head," I admitted. "Let's call that plan B and try to come up with something better."

"What about the men in the other units?" posed Darla. "Maybe they can help."

She rose and headed into Fredric's room, then on to the door connecting the one farther on. I heard her rattle the knob.

"Locked?" I called out.

"Yeah, but I can't be surprised."

She knocked softly, then louder. "Hello, anybody there?" Placing her ear against the wood panel, she listened for a moment, then her shoulders slumped. "Nothing. Either it's vacant or..."

No one wanted to hear the end of that statement.

As Darla returned to us, I could see she was shaken. I feared her burst of determination was about to run dry, which meant it was up to me. Unfortunately, I had nothing.

"Unless we can come up with an alternative, Plan B seems to be it. I know it will be hard for you, Fredric, but I just don't see another way."

Suddenly I felt something brush across my ankles. I cried out and catapulted onto the bed. Was the old motel overrun with rats after all?

A moment later, Maz jumped up beside me with a *prrup*. I couldn't believe my eyes! I gaped at the fluffy old puss, as did Darla and Fredric. Reaching out my hand, I let him push his flat face against it.

"A cat?" Fredric remarked.

"Prin's cat Maz," said Darla. "We met him on the way in."

"You little sneaker," I said to Maz, then I turned to the others. "You know what this means, don't you?"

"That we won't die catless?" Darla suggested.

"No one's going to die. Last time I saw Maz was before Prin locked us in here. He was heading back to the main house. If he's here now, that means he found a way in…"

"And if the cat got in," Fredric finished for me, "then we should be able to get out."

Chapter 27

Cats have been compared to water, in that they seem to be able to flow freely like a liquid, giving them the ability to maneuver through the smallest of spaces.

Maz's miraculous appearance changed everything, and instantly all three of us were up and staring around.

"Did you see where he came from?" I exclaimed, peering this way and that like a nervous cat.

Fredric panned the room. "I didn't notice him till you screamed."

"That wasn't a scream," I argued, "just an exclamation of surprise."

Fredric raised an eyebrow. "It was a scream, Lynley. But no one's blaming you—are we, Darla?" Grinning, he almost seemed like his normal self.

"Not a bit," Darla said, smiling too. Then she sobered and pointed at the door to unit two, Fredric's unit. "Maybe in there? We might have missed something in the dark. Should we look again?"

Fredric's face fell, turning him back into the gaunt stranger. "I'll go," he said bravely.

I touched his arm. "No, I'll go. You and Darla keep on checking in here."

Fredric gave a moan of relief, then turned and went into the little bathroom while Darla made another sweep of the room itself. I was half around the still-frigid space, trying not to picture what it must have been like for

Fredric, all those days in the dark, when I heard him call out.

"Guys, come look at this."

I wasted no time rushing back to see what he had discovered. Darla was already at the bathroom door, staring up.

"Drat!" she exclaimed. "How did I miss it? I searched this whole area, at least I thought I did."

"People forget to look up," said Fredric. "It's a common omission. We found it now—that's what counts."

I squeezed into the tiny room and stared around. There was really nothing to see—toilet, sink, cramped shower stall. Then I felt a breeze on my hair. Where the wall met the ceiling was a narrow window made of glass bricks. One of the bricks was missing.

I felt the shimmer of cat fur on my leg as Maz slipped by. Unlike before, I felt only excitement at the tickle. Sure enough, he was on a mission. He took a little leap onto the sink and then into the square hole left by the missing brick. Turning briefly to give us a sly cat smile, he vaulted outside.

"That's not much help," Darla sighed. "If only we were cats…"

I craned my neck toward the window, but I was too short to see much. "What about the rest of the bricks? If one came out, maybe the others will too."

"Here, let me have a look," Fredric charged.

He moved up close to the wall and began feeling along the sill. It was high, even for him, but he could reach it if he stood on his toes. Maneuvering to grab one of the intact bricks, he gave a great pull, but the thing didn't budge. He tried pushing, then joggling it back and forth. It was awkward work with his arms raised above his head.

Finally he dropped them to his side with a grunt.

"The grout is loose—I can feel it move, but only a little. I wish I had something to dig with."

Darla paused, then pulled up her sleeve to reveal a slim silver bracelet. "Will this help?"

Fredric examined the piece, a half-inch band with cats etched into the metal. Darla turned her wrist, showing the gap at the back of the bracelet and the slightly tapered ends.

"Might work, but I would probably ruin it." He looked at the woman for approval.

Darla slipped it off and handed it over. "Go ahead. It'll do me no good if we don't get out of here."

Fredric didn't hesitate, gouging into the old plaster a little at a time. The bracelet wasn't the most efficient tool, but Fredric wielded it with the passion of a master. I watched the progress like a sports fan viewing a significant play.

After a time, Fredric lowered his arms and slumped against the wall.

"Are you okay?"

He shook his head. "Boy, I've never felt so weak in my life. If I get out of this, the first thing I'm doing is going to the gym."

"*When* we get out of this..." I corrected.

He smiled wanly. "Right, Lynley. *When...*"

Going back to his work, he gave a few more gouges, then grabbed the brick with both hands and worked it back and forth with steadily increasing pressure.

"It's moving!" cried Darla.

I could see it too—a definite wobble. "Can you get it out?"

"I think so."

He worried it even more violently, the sweat beginning to bead on his pale forehead. With a rain of plaster and a grunt from Fredric, it came away and crashed to the floor where it broke into pieces.

Fredric took a step backward, which meant everyone else in the small room did as well.

"The next one will be easier. That one was holding it in."

He started forward, but I held his arm. "Let me clean up the broken glass first. You're barefoot, and you don't want to get cut."

"Good point, but hurry," he hissed. "I have a bad feeling. I think Darla's right—Prin's not going to leave you to rot like the rest of us. She'll be back, and I want to be gone by then."

Darla and Fredric went to sit down while I gathered the remnants of the brick. Instead of shattering, the heavy glass had merely burst into a half-dozen chunks. I picked them up, dropped them in the sink, then dusted off the floor as best I could with the sleeve of my coat.

As I surveyed the room to make sure I hadn't missed a spike, my eye drifted to the window—rough edges there too, but of plaster, not glass. Then I noticed something that made my heart fall. Even with the removal of the twelve-by-twelve bricks, the height of the space could have been no more than fourteen inches, fine for a cat and for young, slim folks, but I would never make it through.

"Ready?" came Fredric's voice from behind me. Seeing his optimistic look, I decided not to say anything just yet.

I stepped aside. "Have at it. Good luck."

The next brick came out easily and in one piece as Fredric had predicted. There was now an escape route for everyone but me.

I took off my coat. "Here, wipe off the plaster with this so you don't get mangled on your way out."

Fredric took the garment and ran it along the ledge, causing a shower of chunks and dust that made me want to sneeze. He started to hand it back to me.

"No, you take it. You're going to need something to cover up all that bare skin once you're outside."

He smiled and slipped on the coat. It was small on him, with the sleeves high on his forearms, but it would do. Then he turned to study the hole.

"It'll be awkward, but it can be done," he muttered, as if to himself. "If we stand on the toilet seat and go at it from that angle, we should be able to…"

He removed the coat once more and pushed it into the space. Balancing on the commode, he hoisted himself up and wriggled through behind it. The process took effort, along with grumbles and a few swears, but he made it. Torso, legs, and finally feet disappeared into the blackness outside. There was a thump as he hit the ground, then his face returned to the hole.

"It's good. There's a brick planter wall—be careful not to hit it when you drop. I'm standing on it." He looked away. "All quiet out here, but hurry. I won't feel safe until I put miles between me and this place."

"And tell the police," I added.

"Yeah, first thing."

Darla was already perched on the toilet, ready to go. Fredric helped her through, and aside from a tear in her pant leg, she was out and down without issue.

"Now you, Lynley," Fredric called through the window.

I didn't move. I wanted to say something, but my voice wouldn't work. I felt like I was choking.

"I... I can't," I finally blurted. "I won't fit."

Fredric stared at me in dismay. "Lynley, you have to. At least try."

But I could see from his face that he knew it wasn't going to happen.

"What's wrong?" I heard Darla say.

"It's Lynley. She can't get out this way. Go around and see if you can open the door from there."

A few moments later I heard the doorknob rattle. Running to the front window, I pulled the curtain aside.

"It's locked... needs a key." Her voice was muffled, but I could see her fear.

Fredric joined her, and we gaped at each other through the glass.

"You go. Get help and come back for me."

"I'm not leaving you," Darla exclaimed.

"Take the car. Get the police. I'll be okay."

Fredric hesitated, then gave me a little salute. "We'll be right back. I promise."

He took Darla's hand and pulled her away.

"But Lynley..."

"It's fine," I called after her. "I'll be fine. Hurry..." I added softly to no one but myself.

I watched them vanish into the shadows, Darla looking back at me as Fredric propelled her along. From my vantage point, I couldn't see the car, so breath held, I awaited some sign they'd succeeded. Then came the double thunk of the car doors. I listened for the engine, but Hybrid cars being notoriously quiet, and the window muffling what little sound there was, I wasn't altogether surprised when it didn't come.

They must have gotten away, I told myself. *They had to have gotten away!*

For an undetermined time, I stood immobile, trying to decide what to do until someone arrived to save me. Who would come first—the police or Prin? If it was Prin, it might be best if she didn't know Darla was gone. The longer I could carry on a charade of normalcy, the longer Darla and Fredric would have to get help.

That was assuming Prin hadn't heard the car start up and leave.

I put the thought out of my mind and crossed the room once more. Shutting the door to the bathroom to block the telltale breeze from the open window, I rehearsed my story. I would say Darla was in there, sick or constipated—something to account for her absence.

I closed the door to the adjoining unit, hefted the broken credenza upright, and pushed it back in place. With a pillow, I swept the shards of mirror under the bed. I turned on the small bedside lamp and flicked off the overhead light, casting the room into dim so Prin wouldn't notice the broken mirror, at least not first thing.

Taking deep breaths to quell the fear and anxiety that were coursing through me with the regularity of a heartbeat, I sat down in the easy chair to wait.

Chapter 28

Your cat probably knows you better than you know her.

Despite the tension, or maybe because of it, I found myself drifting and was nearly asleep when I heard the key in the lock. I vaulted to my feet—this was it! Would Prin be angry? Crazy? Violent? What would she do when she figured out Darla had escaped? And Fredric, her victim—she wouldn't be happy about losing that one.

I grabbed the trusty bible and ran to the door—if I caught her unawares, I might be able to get in a good whack and slip out while she was recovering. There were problems with that approach, such as where I would go once out. Darla and Fredric had taken the car. I could hardly outrun Prin into town, and the idea of hiding in the woods with the bears and the coyotes, to say nothing of the spiders, ants, and centipedes, didn't thrill me either. In the end, I stayed put, holding the big book in front of me like a shield.

The door opened, and in trotted Maz with Prin following behind. She seemed surprised to see me lurking, but the bewilderment lasted only a moment. Pushing the door shut, she calmly relocked it from the inside, then dropped the key into the pocket of her oversized jeans where it clinked against something else metal. I hoped it wasn't a weapon.

Stepping past me, she gazed around the darkened room.

"Darla is in the bathroom," I lied.

Prin turned, her face blank. "No, she isn't."

"Yes, she..." I faltered, then grasped the full implication of her words.

"That's right," Prin hissed. "Your getaway plan backfired. Now she and... that *man*—" She spat the word, *man*, as if he were the devil himself. "—are incapacitated."

"What do you mean? Are they alright?"

She narrowed her eyes, then gave a sigh. "Yeah, they're fine. I locked the man in the laundry room where he can't do any more harm. Darla is resting quietly in my bedroom."

"What did you do to her?"

"This isn't your show, Lynley-from-Friends-of-Felines—it's mine."

I held up one hand, the bible still clutched tight in the other. "Okay, alright. It's your show. What do you want from us?"

She cocked her head. "To tell you the truth, I really don't know."

Crossing to the easy chair, she plunked herself down as if exhausted from a hard day's work. Maybe kidnapping took more effort than I'd imagined.

I moved to the bed and perched on the edge in case I had to run, though I doubted I'd get the chance, and as I'd worked out previously, there was no place to go.

"Tell me," I said with faux sympathy. "Maybe I can help."

"Help?" she barked back. "You must be kidding. Everything was good until you showed up—you and Dee. Now it's a mess, and it's all your fault."

"Our fault?" That was a new one. "How can it be our fault?"

"Isn't it obvious? I can't harm you—you've done nothing wrong aside from being cat-curious. I get it. You discovered an enigma, and you just couldn't let it go."

"Something like that," I confessed, deciding it wouldn't hurt to agree with her, since she was essentially correct.

Maz hopped up on her lap and smushed his face against her hand. Without thought, she began stroking the luxurious fur.

"I always knew there would be an end to this," Prin muttered, as if to herself. "Crime isn't sustainable." She turned to me. "That's right, Lynley. I knew what I was doing all along—committing a crime. I'm not crazy—I shouldn't have taken those men. But I couldn't help myself. It was..." She licked her lips. In a cat, lip-licking was a sign of stress—maybe the same was true for her. "It was necessary for the salvation of my soul."

She hung her head, and suddenly my perception flip-flopped. Instead of the ruthless villain, I saw only a little girl, hurting and hollow. What had happened to her to make her take such a dive?

She was now petting the cat as if her life depended on it, the strokes coming hard and fast. Maz had enough and wriggled out of her grasp. Hopping from the chair to the bed, he came to investigate the other occupant in the room—me. I held out my hand for him to sniff, and he must have approved, because he plunked himself down beside me and began to groom.

Prin's eyes followed the cat's every move. "He likes you," she said, sounding melancholy. I was beginning to see that sadness was the woman's default setting.

"Who hurt you?" I asked quietly.

Her eyes met mine as she uttered one word:

"Everyone."

* * *

Without warning, Prin leapt from her chair and began to pace the room. Crossing to the bathroom and flinging open the door, she eyed the broken window with nothing short of hatred. As she turned, her gaze lit on the cracks in the wall and the connecting door behind.

"So that's how he did it," she fumed, not so much to me as to herself. "That dirty piece of…"

With a strangled cry, she went for the credenza, hefted it into the air as if it were nothing, and flung it crashing to the ground. In two long strides, she was at the window, grabbing the curtains and yanking them down. I was pretty sure that when she ran out of furniture to abuse, she would turn her rage on me.

I was wrong. Her next move, shocking in its intensity, was to fall to her knees and begin to sob.

Wrapping her arms around herself, she crumpled onto her side, her head resting on the broken leg of the credenza. This was my chance! In her present, passive state, it wouldn't take much to wrestle the key out of her pocket and make a run for it. The temper tantrum had scared me, and she was strong—no doubt stronger than I was—but I didn't think she'd put up a fight now. Did she even care? As I watched her suffering, I somehow doubted it.

But instead of executing my rather dubious plan, I remained where I was.

"Prin?"

She rolled over and trained her tear-rimmed eyes on me. "What?"

"Well, are you alright?"

She stared blankly, blinked a couple of times, then without comment, pulled herself upright, got to her feet, and disappeared into the bathroom. I heard the sound of running water, and when she returned, only the red of her dampened face betrayed her earlier weakness.

She flopped into the easy chair with an *oof*, then reached over to pet Maz who was still on the bed. Prin's outburst hadn't bothered the cat one bit, which led me to believe such behavior might be a common occurrence.

"Prin," I said as evenly as I could muster, "It's time to end this. You know it can't go on. Let Darla and me go. As you said, we've done you no harm."

She didn't agree, but she didn't say no, which I took as a positive sign.

"And Fredric..." I added tentatively.

She fired me a look. "*You* haven't harmed me, but that man... He... He..."

He what? What could Fredric have done to hurt this woman so deeply?

"No," she continued. "The men stay. They need to understand. They need to learn."

"The I-5 Lost Boys?"

"Ha," she grunted. "The news media came up with that one. But they're not boys and they're not lost—they're here. I know it's breaking the law, but they must be eschewed."

Eschewed—an old fashioned word I'd rarely, if ever, heard spoken in common conversation, but I knew what it meant: shunned.

"But why? Why must they be... eschewed? Come on, Prin. Help me understand."

Instead of answering directly, she stood and held her arms out wide. "Am I that gross, that disgusting?" She turned in a circle, then let her arms fall to her sides in a defeated gesture. "I'm kind to animals. I'm helpful to others. I'm a good person—don't I deserve to be loved like everyone else?"

I didn't want to bring up the fact that good people don't go around kidnapping, so I said nothing. The question turned out to be rhetorical.

"I've been rejected my whole life, Lynley." She grabbed Maz and fell back onto the chair. The cat settled lovingly—no rejection there, and I could see why she preferred cats to people.

"My birth mother dumped me at an adoption agency as soon as she got the chance," Prin snorted. "My adoptive parents belonged to a group with a system of strict laws. If I didn't do as I was told, they would put me in my room, sometimes for days. If I broke the rules, they'd ignore me, act as if I didn't exist. I can still hear Dada's voice—'If you keep this up, Princess, you're bound to get a shunning.'"

"That's terrible," I remarked honestly.

"The older I got, the more it happened. I began to feel dead inside. I moved out the day I turned eighteen and never looked back."

She lifted her gaze from Maz to me, her eyes pleading yet harsh at the same time.

"But the rest of the world wasn't much better. Guys are cruel, Lynley. They say they care... say they love you... then they change. They ghost you, just like my parents did, or they bolt and never come back. I got sick of being rejected. Sick of it!" she cried out, then she cleared her throat. "That's when I decided to stop playing the victim. It was time I turned their actions back on them."

"Prin, your parents treated you horribly—there's no denying that—but it's no reason to take it out on others.

We all get rejected sometimes—it's part of relationships. You can't expect everyone you like to feel the same way about you."

Her eyes squinted and her jaw clenched. "But every… single… time?"

Suddenly my temper flared. "So you got hurt and paid them back by drugging them and… what? Throwing them in a cold, dark room to suffer?"

She nodded vigorously. "Pretty much. How else will they know how it feels?"

"You've got five men locked in a motel. What did you hope to accomplish?"

She shrugged. "Four. One stole my old truck and got away."

Gerald Sullivan. Picturing the emaciated figure wrapped in the blue tarp, I got even madder.

"That man, Prin… the one who escaped…" I took a deep breath. I was about to go out on a limb, but I needed to do something to jar her from her pity party. "He's dead."

"What?"

"Haven't you seen the news? He didn't make it," I said frankly. "By the time he was found, he was too far gone to recover. What you're doing to these men isn't teaching them a lesson—it's killing them. Prin, like it or not, you are a murderer."

Prin had gone absolutely still. I waited, my heartbeat ticking away the seconds like a grandfather clock.

Finally she made a spitting sound. "And I should care why? That's what happens to people who are cruel and heartless."

And what about you, you predator? I wanted to shout but stopped myself. Hurling more accusations would get me nowhere, so instead, I went in a different direction.

"You may not have cared about the men, but their cats were another story, am I right?"

She looked surprised.

"That's what gave you away—Fredric's kitten Tarzan. I was at Darla's house when she brought him in, and I recognized him immediately. Your story about rehoming unadoptable strays from the shelter fell apart then and there."

"What was I supposed to do?" she shot back. "I couldn't let a cat suffer for something a man had done."

"And what had Fredric done, aside from be nice to you and take you out for coffee?"

"He told you that?"

I nodded.

"Did he tell you he invited me back to his place? You know what that means. But when we got there, he shunned me like all the rest."

"You must have misunderstood his intentions. Fredric is involved with my granddaughter. He would never have led you on that way."

"What do you know, old woman?" she grunted.

The insult hit and stung, but there was no use in arguing.

"And the others? You rescued their cats too."

She nodded. "I had to—they couldn't survive on their own. But I couldn't turn them in to the shelter. If they were chipped, they would have been traced."

"So you gave them to Darla."

For the first time since I'd met Prin, all the attitude fell away, and she shot me a guileless smile. "Darla was so nice about it. She never questioned, never balked. She's totally committed to helping cats, you know, whatever it takes."

With a pause, the smile faded. "I felt badly for deceiving her. I'd hoped there would come a time when we could be friends, and I could tell her the truth."

"You are friends," I found myself saying. "Darla cares about you."

"Maybe once, but she'll change her mind about that now, won't she?" Prin said flatly. "The things I've done. I know I've treated her poorly."

"I don't think she'll turn her back on you. She's stuck up for you all along. Maybe there's still hope for a friendship."

"I doubt it," Prin threw out sullenly.

"Now who's rejecting who? Give her a chance. Tell her what you've told me. See what happens."

Prin was thoughtful, her fingers woven into Maz's silky fur. I had no idea what was going on in that convoluted mind of hers. Prin was an enigma, and her story, tragic. A woman who had suffered being shunned from birth but who felt no qualms about turning the same cruel behavior on others. A person who cared little for human life but loved cats to the point of obsession. She could toss furniture across the room, then break down and cry like a baby. I had no way of knowing what she might do next or what effect my words could have upon her, but I said them anyway:

"It's over, Prin. Let it go and move on with your life."

There was a long pause, then she said so softly I could barely hear, "You're right. It's time."

But still she hesitated, petting Maz tenderly—head to tail, head to tail. The cat snuggled against her, a bond so deep it couldn't be broken.

With Maz in her arms, she stood. Crossing slowly to

where I sat, she pulled him away from her chest and handed him to me.

"Take good care of him, Lynley. He's the best kitty ever."

Then Prin turned on her heel and went to the door. Unlocking it, she stood in the doorway.

"I'm afraid I'm going to have to lock you in again, Lynley. I need time to get away. But don't worry — someone will come for you shortly."

With that she turned and was gone. I heard the key click in the lock once more, then silence.

Still holding Maz, I rose and crossed to the now-curtainless window. I stared outside, but there was no sign of Prin. Then a car engine roared to life. Headlamps flicked on, shooting twin beams into the forest. The lights began to bob through the trees like will-o-the-wisps as Prin made her escape. Where she thought she was going was a mystery to me. She must have known she would be caught or else she would have taken her cat.

I looked at Maz, who was blinking his golden eyes as if trying to hold back tears. Cats may not cry, but they do feel grief. Did Maz understand what Prin had done? Did he know what Prin was doing now?

I turned back to the darkened window, feeling a sense of deep melancholy, even though I knew my ordeal was nearly over. Prin said someone would come for us. For the first time since we'd met, I believed her.

Chapter 29

Cat Tuna Crackers
   1 can 6 oz. undrained tuna in water
   1 cup cornmeal
   1 cup wheat flour
   Water
Mix all ingredients in bowl. Roll out to ¼" thickness and cut into squares. Bake on a cookie sheet at 350° for 20 minutes or until golden. Cool before serving.

"I-5 Kidnapper Apprehended," read the headline of the Oregonian newspaper. "Victims Recovering at OHSU."

Yes, I still buy a real printed paper every so often, and this was one of those times. I'd walked down to the kiosk first thing that morning, a brisk trek in pouring rain, but was now comfortably back on my couch, feet up, with Dirty Harry curled on my lap. Reading the paper was about all I could cope with. The encounter with the sad but lethal Prin had been a nightmare, and like any traumatic experience, just because it was over didn't mean it was done.

Prin had fulfilled her promise—sometime after her surprising departure, the police arrived. They quickly assessed the situation and set us free, Darla and me to a police cruiser to be interviewed, and Fredric, along with the three other captured men, to the hospital in Vancouver. I rustled up a carrier for Maz and told the officer in charge to watch for other cats in case Prin had more than just the one. I suppose I was still looking for those promised tabbies and the big Maine Coon.

In halting remarks, Darla and I caught up in the cruiser. She told me how Prin had caught her and Fredric on their way to the car, herding them into the house and locking them in separate rooms. I recounted Prin's tantrum, confessions, and unexpected surrender. Around dawn, we were finally given leave to return home. That was two days earlier. Now, as I relished the simple pleasure of lounging with Harry, I couldn't think of a better place to be or anything more I wanted from life.

I heard a tap on my door, then a key in the lock.

"Hello, dear," my mother called from the hallway.

"Come on in, Mum. I'm resting. Still resting…"

"That's why I used my key." Carol shed her coat in the hallway and hung it on the peg by the door. "I didn't want you to have to get up."

"Is it still raining?"

"Raining again," she corrected. "It stopped for a good half hour, but now it's back. The Weather Kitty app on my phone says it will pass soon though. Then we might even get a bit of sun."

"That would be nice. The darkness is smothering me." I shuddered. I may have been accustomed to Portland's seasons of gray, but that didn't mean I always liked them.

Carol came and plopped down on the ottoman beside me. "Are you feeling better, dear?"

I nodded. "Loads. But I'm glad I don't have to do anything right now."

"Except to get ready for Harry's party," Carol said, scritching the big tuxedo cat on his fat black cheek.

"Thankfully that won't require much preparation. Harry will be happy with whatever we do as long as he gets treats."

"And speaking of treats…" Carol dug in her oversized tote and drew out a squarish book with a tattered teal cover.

"Your mother's cookbook?"

She nodded. "Guess what I found when I was looking for a cupcake recipe."

"Lime Jell-O salad? Aspic on toast?"

She smiled like a mischievous cat. "Nope."

"Chicken a la King? Spam fricassee?"

"Not even close, but you'll never get it, so I suppose I'll have to tell you." Dramatic pause. "Cat treats! There's a recipe for something called Tuna Crackers—for cats!"

"Really? I know your mum loved cats but…"

"We grew up with cats," Carol said fondly, "though I can't remember her ever cooking for them."

She opened the dogeared volume and thumbed through to a bookmarked page. "It looks easy enough. Want to give it a try?"

"Sure, why not?" I gazed around at my clowder, all of whom were sitting, playing, or sleeping nearby. "I'm sure someone will eat them."

"I'll make some extra for Maz. Have you heard how he's settling in with your cat sitting client?"

"Darla texted this morning. She's got Maz in her bedroom for now, but he seems happy."

"And Darla herself?"

"She says she'd doing fine, but I think deep down, the whole experience shook her. She trusted Prin."

"It must have been a shock to find out her mentor was a villainous criminal."

"I'm sure it was, but she's not giving up on Prin. She's already talked to her. Apparently Prin wants to start a program to connect prison inmates with behavior-challenged cats, and Darla is planning to help her."

"What about the kidnap victims' cats? Will they go back to their original people?"

"Yes, Webster, Hans, and Newberry will go home once the men are out of the hospital. Billy, Gerald Sullivan's boy, is being adopted by Gerald's sister who loves him. Sheba the FIP kitten is going to a family who have treated FIP cats before. They'll take her through the rest of her treatment and love her for the rest of her life. That brings Darla's cat count down to a manageable level, even with the addition of Maz."

"Are you going to continue cat sitting for her?"

I shook my head. "I think my career as a cat sitter is over. I enjoyed it, but I have enough cat duties right here at home."

There was a knock on the door. Carol jumped to get it before I could move.

"Hi, Grandmother," called Seleia from the front hall.

She moved into the entranceway, where she was joined by Fredric. The young man looked slightly thinner than normal, but his smile was bright.

Hand in hand, the two came to sit on the sofa where we went through much the same, *How are you? I'm fine*, greeting as I'd done with my mother. Then I turned to Fredric.

"I thought you were in the hospital."

"They discharged me last night. There's nothing wrong with me other than a few days of involuntary fasting."

"He makes light," Seleia put in, "but I know it must have been horrible." Her look said it all—concern, empathy, love. Whatever thoughts she may have had about seeing other boys were far from her mind now.

"Awful," Carol shook her head as she came up behind them. "Not knowing when you'd get out."

"*If* I'd get out," Fredric said with a wince.

Seleia leaned over and kissed the young man's cheek. "But you did get out, and now you're okay and everything's going to be good from here on in."

I knew that was simplistic thinking, but judging by Seleia's manner, whatever lingering trauma Fredric might have, he wouldn't be going through it alone.

Fredric banished the haunted look that threatened his smile. "The other guys are okay too. I talked to them in the hospital. They all said the docs are expecting complete recoveries."

Carol picked up the teal cookbook and her tote full of ingredients. "That's wonderful. Now I have a pressing engagement with your oven, Lynley. Seleia, would you like to help me?"

Seleia gave a questioning look.

"Your great grandmother has discovered the family recipe for cat treats. She's going to make them for Harry's party."

Carol gave a wave and withdrew into the kitchen.

"Let me know if you need anything," I called after her, "as long as it doesn't entail me getting up off the couch."

Seleia glanced at Fredric. "You don't mind?"

He laughed. "I think I can survive for a few minutes without you watching over me like a mother cat. Lynley will see that I don't wither away."

"Well, if you're sure…"

"I'm sure. Now go help your Granna."

I watched his gaze follow her out of the room. "Looks like you two have patched things up."

"Yeah, we talked it out. It's not like we're engaged or

anything—neither of us are ready for that yet—but the idea of us dating other people doesn't work either. We're going to see what happens from here."

Harry snuggled deeper into my lap. "Sounds good. I'm glad."

"And you, Lynley?" He turned his hazel eyes on me. "You're really okay?"

"I do wish people would stop asking me that," I snapped. "Sorry," I quickly apologized. "It's just such a loaded question. Friends have been calling and texting, asking the same thing—am I okay. What choice do I have but to say I'm fine?"

I adjusted Harry a little higher on my lap. "But sometimes I just want to scream, *No, I'm a mess. I'm anxious and disappointed. I'm confused and scared. I've been to the dark side, and now I can't find the light.*"

"Is that true? Are you still suffering?"

"No, not really, but I'm not *fine* either. I don't know what I am."

Fredric took my hand. "You and me both. I need to keep up a good front for Seleia, but sometimes it's hard, and sometimes it's impossible. That's when I make an excuse and go off by myself until it passes."

I squeezed his hand back. "How about we be each other's grumble buddies? We don't have to tell anyone else, but when we start feeling troubled, we text or call. You can tell me whatever you need to without judgment, and vice versa."

"That sounds like a great idea. I could use a—what did you call it? A *grumble buddy* right about now."

"Then it's settled."

"What's settled?" Seleia asked, coming back into the room.

We both blinked up at her like cats who have done something naughty. Thankfully we were saved by the bell, literally.

"Can you get that, dear?" I'm trying to see how long I can stay on this couch without lifting a finger."

Seleia hopped into the hallway to answer the door, and I gave Fredric a wink. "Grumble buddies," I whispered. "Don't forget."

"I won't," the young man whispered back. "And thanks."

"It's Frannie," Seleia announced.

"Come on in, Frannie. Harry and I are being lazy."

"Cat on Lap syndrome?" Frannie said as she entered.

"*Birthday Cat* on Lap," I replied, stroking the black and white fur. "I can't believe he's seventeen!"

"I know," said Frannie. "I dressed for the occasion." She stripped off her Kate Spade faux patent raincoat to reveal a flouncy cat-print party dress. Raising a cultured eyebrow, she asked, "What do you think?"

"You win the costume contest," I said with a smile.

"Oh, Lynley," Frannie huffed, but I knew she took the joke.

She reached down and gave the old boy a pet, which he answered with a purrumph. "Happy Birthday, big fella, and many happy returns of the day."

Then she turned her attention on me. "How are…"

I held up a hand. "Stop right there. I'm getting by, thanks for asking. I love you. Now let's talk about something else."

Frannie dropped her purse on a chair and sat on the end of the couch by my feet. Hermione appeared out of nowhere and jumped onto her lap where she curled up to nap.

"I'd better get back to Granna before she destroys your kitchen," said Seleia.

"And I'll come supervise," Fredric added jovially, back to his unflappable self.

Frannie sniffed the air as the couple disappeared toward the back of the house.

"Tuna," I affirmed. "Carol's making cat treats from an old family recipe."

Frannie raised a perfectly painted eyebrow. "Your mother never ceases to amaze me."

"Nor me," I replied.

Frannie set to petting Hermione, tracing the paisley swirls in her fur. "I ran into Denny at the shelter. He sends his regrets. He's working and won't make Harry's birthday party, but he told me to tell you that things are going well for that hoarder you helped him with, Judy Smith. They got her house cleaned up, and she's going to counseling. She may be able to keep two cats, a bonded pair, under supervision of the investigations team. I gather she's taking it seriously, a second chance."

"I'm glad to hear it. With so many animals in need, I understand how people get carried away trying to save them all."

For a moment, the conversation lapsed, and we sat in silence, the comfortable kind that happens between friends.

"I know you don't want to talk about it," Frannie said finally, "but you've been through something major, and I need to know if there is anything I can do. I got the gist of the story from Carol, but it sounds like you had a dreadful scare, held in that awful motel all by yourself."

"I wasn't by myself—Darla and Fredric were there most of the time. And the motel wasn't awful, just quaint. I think it had been abandoned for quite a while. How Prin came to be living there is a mystery."

I heard the ding of a timer, then the oven door opening and closing. The scent of baking filled the air, with only a slight aroma of fish.

I sighed. "But you're right. It was scary. I still have a lot of mixed emotions. The thing I keep coming back to is how abysmal it must have been for Prin."

"For Prin, the woman who kidnapped you and abducted those poor men?" Frannie exclaimed. "How can you say that?"

"I don't mean now, the kidnapping part. She was already traumatized by the time she made those decisions. No, I'm thinking of her early life. She grew up in some sort of cult family with strict rules—if the poor little girl misbehaved, they would punish her by acting as if she didn't exist. Can you imagine how dreadful that must have been?"

"I can only guess." Frannie shook her head. "I grew up in a loving home."

"So did I." As if on cue, I heard friendly laughter from the kitchen. "But Prin never knew that sort of love. Her concept of relationships was skewed by her early experiences, so when she was attracted to someone and they didn't respond the same way, she felt like she was being shunned all over again. It broke her. She wanted payback. And she got it the only way she knew how."

"I see what you mean. I hope she can get the help she needs now that she's safely incarcerated."

"Is the birthday boy ready?" Carol called, emerging from the kitchen with a tray of nicely browned squares. Sprigs of parsley rested decoratively at each end.

"Ta-da!" she announced, placing the tray on the

ottoman. "All cooled off and ready to eat."

Harry, awakened by the smell, gave a sniff, then another. Without further ado, he rose from my lap and stepped over to the fare. He licked at a particularly delicious-looking cracker, then began crunching enthusiastically.

"You've got a hit," said Fredric, standing behind Seleia who was watching the old cat with unabashed love.

Carol beamed. "Maybe I should start making them commercially. I could sell them at the Pet Pantry. Homemade and organic? Small, senior woman-owned business? Why, that could be my new career."

Harry seemed to agree, and as she and Seleia passed out the treats to the other cats who had been drawn to the enticing scent, she received even more rave reviews.

Harry had finished his cracker and went hunting for more. Carol placed another in front of him, then retired the tray to a high shelf. "That's enough for now, Harry. We don't want you to yak all over your birthday gifts."

"Speaking of…" I announced. "Seleia, will you grab that box from behind you?"

Seleia passed me the flat cardboard box. I removed the lid revealing a layer of white tissue paper. Pulling up a corner, I showed the humans the bounty.

"It's a Treasure Box—toys, rattle balls, sparklies, and kicker pillows, all dusted with catnip. A volunteer at Friends of Felines makes them, and the proceeds go to the shelter."

I tucked the tissue back in place and set the box on the floor. Harry was down to inspect it in a heartbeat. With unabashed enthusiasm, he clawed through the flimsy paper, rubbed against it, then rolled over in a kittenish fashion, one of the bright catnip kickers grasped between his paws. Everyone laughed to see the old cat playing like a kitten.

Harry picked out each toy in turn, then when all that was left in the box was a dusting of catnip, he stalked over to his favorite bed in the TV cabinet for a well-deserved nap, and the party was over.

Seleia and Fredric put on coats and retired to the garden to enjoy the moment of sunshine the Weather Kitty had promised. Carol, Frannie, and I sat in the remains of birthday chaos, talking about nothing in particular.

Finally Frannie rose and gathered her things.

"I'm sorry, Lynley, I have to take off. My quilting group is meeting in an hour, and I need to pick up some squares from the fabric store."

"I didn't know you were a quilter," said Carol.

"Beginner. I do know how to sew, but I've never tried quilting before. A friend thought I might be interested in this group. They work exclusively on feline designs."

"Cat quilting? That sounds like fun."

"There's still space open in the class," Frannie hinted.

"Even if I could make it off this couch," I replied, "there's no way I'd be ready in an hour. But it does sound tempting."

Frannie said her goodbyes and went off to the class. Carol slipped into the kitchen to clean up. Harry moved from his bed to my lap. I lay back on the couch pillows and closed my eyes. As I started to drift, I envisioned swaths of cat print fabric swirling like banners in the wind. Then they came together, a hand-stitched quilt with the center design of a beautiful black and white cat.

Afterword

The Story of an FIP Crusader

As told to Mollie Hunt by Peter Cohen of *House of Nekko/ZenByCat*

Peter Cohen loves cats. For the past thirty-plus years, he has made a home for them. And not just any home—check out his online videos to see the gorgeous, cat-centric rooms! Among those fabulous blues, teals, and greens, you will find the cats lounging in luxury, nearly thirty of them!

Peter's journey with cats began the way it does for most of us, adopting cats from a local shelter. His goal, to make a home for those cats, meant learning all he could about them. When a kitten named Peanut came into his life, only to get sick and die, Peter was devastated. The veterinarian told him Peanut had contracted a nearly-always fatal disease called *feline infectious peritonitis* (FIP), but that it was rare. Peter thought he would never have to go through that anguish again.

Then came Miss Bean. When this kitten began to exhibit symptoms of FIP, Peter was not so quick to give up. That's when he discovered Dr. Niels Pedersen of UC Davis, a move that would change Peter's life forever.

The doctor was doing a promising clinical trial to treat FIP with a human antiviral drug. Miss Bean was accepted into the study where she responded well until she had the seizure that killed her. Still, Peter was encouraged. For a time, there had been hope.

Through Miss Bean's journey to cure her FIP, Peter learned of Smokey. Smokey had been accepted into the same UC Davis treatment program, and *House of Nekko* adopted him to help him in his fight. Smokey responded well to the UC Davis trial drug. All his symptoms disappeared by the end of the 2nd week, and his blood tests showed him within normal ranges. Smokey has been in complete remission since he finished his regimen, and his doctors now consider him cured of FIP.

With the success of Smokey, Peter felt motivated to help carry on this vision of a cure for FIP and asked Dr. Pedersen what he could do to help. The answer was funding. While no one wants cats to die, many people were reluctant to invest in a drug with an unforeseeable future. Research takes money.

Peter was already well on the road to cat internet celebrity with his fantastic cat house. He took up the cause, turning his efforts to raising awareness of FIP, gathering supporters for FIP research, and helping set up groups that assist cat owners in obtaining and implementing the unapproved treatment.

Thanks to the progress Peter and those groups have made, FIP has been upgraded from an *always fatal* to a *treatable* disease. Cats are surviving this disease! Over 100,000 cats from around the world have been saved through this treatment which works an astounding 85% to 90% of the time. Unfortunately, the high cost of the drug keeps it out of reach of many cat owners. The fact it isn't FDA approved further hinders its acceptance.

There is much work to be done. Research supported by ZenByCat is working on a second, unrelated drug to treat FIP, one that will be approved by the FDA. The new study is halfway through a seven-year trial, so there may be good news soon. In the meantime, ZenByCat and FIP Warriors are here to help.

I asked Peter why he devoted his life to saving cats and

FIP cats in particular. His answer was simple and candid.

"Some people can filter out all the bad things going on around us, but I'm not one of them. There are so many human crises about which I can do nothing—I struggle with that. But cats are different. When you save a cat, you save its entire world."

Saving cats is a simple joy for Peter, and he has a lot to be proud of. FIP has gone from a disease where all cats die to one where they can be saved, and his work has played a part in that accomplishment. To the unpretentious Peter Cohen, it's purely "paying it forward," but for anyone whose life has been touched by FIP, his optimism, hope, and relentless spirit is a beacon of light.

ZENBYCAT

ZenByCat is a 501(c)(3) nonprofit organization whose mission is to raise awareness and money to find a cure for Feline Infectious Peritonitis (FIP).

HOUSE OF NEKKO

House Of Nekko is dedicated to showing how living with cats improves both human and feline lives. All of the cats living in House Of Nekko were adopted from shelters, many considered "undesirable" by other adopters for one reason or another. Some were traumatized kittens, not playful and afraid of humans, so nobody wanted them. They deserve to be loved too, which is why they now live at The House Of Nekko.

FIP WARRIORS

FIP Warriors is a global network made up of cat lovers, breeders, and rescuers—many of whom have been through treatment with their own cats. They help owners of sick cats get medication quickly, share notes on the best "brands" to purchase, and teach owners how to give daily subcutaneous injections to their cats,

What is FIP?

"Feline infectious peritonitis (FIP) is a viral disease of cats caused by certain strains of a virus called the feline coronavirus*. Most strains do not cause significant disease, but in approximately 10 percent of cats, one or more mutations of the virus can result in white blood cells becoming infected with the virus and spreading it throughout the cat's body. When this occurs, the virus is referred to as the FIPV. An intense inflammatory reaction to FIPV occurs around vessels in the tissues where these infected cells locate, often in the abdomen, kidney, or brain. It is this interaction between the body's own immune system and the virus that is responsible for the development of FIP.

Once a cat develops clinical FIP, the disease is usually progressive and almost always fatal without therapy that has recently become available, but that has yet to be approved to treat FIP in cats by the Food and Drug Administration (FDA).

Until recently, FIP was considered to be a non-treatable disease. While there are still some uncertainties regarding the long-term effectiveness of recently-identified antiviral drugs, studies in both the laboratory and in client-owned cats with naturally occurring FIP suggest that a drug may ultimately prove to be an effective treatment option for FIP. This drug is currently not FDA-approved, however, and while there are a number of sources offering it for sale, anecdotal reports suggest that the products being provided by some of these sources vary widely in both accuracy of reported drug concentration and purity. It is very important to discuss the risks, benefits, and evolving acquisition and regulatory issues with your veterinarian."

—Cornell Feline Health Center

*FIP virus is not infectious to humans and different from the coronavirus that causes COVID-19 in people.

A Note from the Author

Thanks so much for reading my tenth Crazy Cat Lady Mystery, *Cat House*. I hope you enjoyed it. If you did, please consider leaving a review on your favorite book and social media sites. Reviews help indie authors such as myself to gain recognition in the literary jungle. Thank you in advance for your consideration.

Want more cozy cat mysteries? Look for more books in my **Crazy Cat Lady** series. Don't worry—the books need not be read in order. Just pick a plot that interests you and start reading.

"...Each book drew me right into the story and kept me intrigued and guessing all the way." —Catwoods Porch Party

Or check out my **Tenth Life Paranormal Mysteries** involving a septuagenarian, a ghost cat, and a small coastal town.

"This is the sort of cozy mystery that you like to curl up with on a rainy day with a cup of tea." —Verified Reader

For sci-fantasy fans, there is my **Cat Seasons Tetralogy**—Cats saving the world!

"Mollie weaves a story that blurs the lines of mythology, spiritualism, mysticism, science and reality that took me into another world." — Ramona D. Marek MS Ed, CWA Author

About the Author

Cat Writer Mollie Hunt is the award-winning author of two cozy series, the **Crazy Cat Lady Mysteries**, featuring a sixty-something cat shelter volunteer who finds more trouble than a cat in catnip, and the **Tenth Life Paranormal Mysteries** involving a ghost cat. Her **Cat Seasons Sci-Fantasy Tetralogy** presents extraordinary cats saving the world. She also pens a bit of cat poetry.

Mollie is a member of the Willamette Writers, Oregon Writers' Colony, Sisters in Crime, the Cat Writers' Association, and Northwest Independent Writers Association (NIWA). She lives in Portland, Oregon with her husband and a varying number of cats. Like her cat lady character, she is a grateful shelter volunteer.

About the Cover Art

"Fireside Cat," by Leslie Cobb

"That one doesn't have a story. It's just a made-up cat in a setting loosely based on a room I saw in a magazine and liked."
—Leslie Cobb

© 2002 *Leslie Cobb* www.lesliecobb.com

Made in the USA
Monee, IL
10 September 2023